WITHDRAWN

THREE KEYS

ALSO BY KELLY YANG

FRONT DESK

THREE KEYS

A **FRONT DESK** NOVEL

KELLY YANG

SCHOLASTIC PRESS / NEW YORK

Library of Congress Cataloging-in-Publication Data available
ISBN 978-1-338-59138-5

10 9 8 7 6 5 4 3 2 1   20 21 22 23 24

Printed in the U.S.A.   23
First edition, September 2020
Book design by Maeve Norton

TO ALL THE DREAMERS.

CHAPTER 1

A very wise person once told me that there are two roller coasters in America — one for the poor and one for the rich. I've only been on one of those roller coasters, and I thought I was never going to get off. But as I watched my best friend, Lupe, decorate the Calivista Motel pool with silver and gold lights, a smile stretched across my face. The lights were the kind you put up at your house at Christmas. Even though it was the middle of August and the summer sun beat down on us, it sure *felt* like Christmas. We were owners now. We had bought the motel from Mr. Yao, and we were finally going to run it our way!

"A little to the left!" Mrs. T, one of the weeklies, called, pointing to the *BBQ at the Pool* sign. She and the other weeklies — Hank, Mrs. Q, Fred, and Billy Bob — were also helping set up. They were our regular customers at the motel, but they were so much more — they were family. Hank smiled at the sign. The barbecue was his idea. It was part of his "friendlier and warmer" rebranding of the Calivista. And it was going to be *delicious*. We were having Hank's tangy-sweet baby back ribs, Fred's corn on the cob, and my mom's fried rice.

Hank adjusted the sign and we all stood back to admire it. Lupe's dad, José, gave a holler and a thumbs-up from the roof. I waved back at José. Ever since we took over the motel, he'd been working almost exclusively at the Calivista, which meant I'd gotten to hang out with Lupe all summer long.

My mom rushed out from the manager's quarters with a large cooler full of ice, with my dad trailing after her.

"Don't take that out so early," my dad cautioned. "The ice is going to melt!"

My mom placed the cooler beside the table with the napkins and drinks. "Then I'll just run out and get some more!" she said.

You'd think now that we were making more money, my parents would stop bickering. But every morning, my dad still pours the cooking oil he saved from the previous night's dinner into the breakfast pan, saying "Don't waste" in Chinese. And he still pulls a square from the toilet paper roll to wipe his nose, instead of using a Kleenex. It's like he doesn't believe any of this is real—that if he doesn't save every penny, it'll all disappear.

I walked over to the white plastic pool chairs where my dad sat and bent down next to him.

"We're on the good roller coaster now, Dad," I told him. "Things are going to be different, you'll see."

He reached out and ruffled my hair.

Soon, the pool started filling up with guests. Besides the customers, my mom had invited a few of the immigrant investors who had chipped in to help buy the motel. She'd also invited some of the paper investors, the people who invested money but rarely came around. Instead, every month, we mailed them a check and a report. I *loved* writing the reports. As I squeezed by them, I heard them chatting about what a great summer it had been and how investing in the Calivista was the best decision they've ever made, and it made me so proud.

At the drinks and napkins table, a few of our customers were talking about the governor's race here in California.

"Have you seen the ads?" one of the guests, Mr. Dunkin (room 15), asked his neighbor, Mr. Miller (room 16). I looked over to see the reaction. Lately, you couldn't miss Governor Wilson on television. He was running for reelection against a woman, Kathleen Brown. His campaign ads showed people running across the US-Mexico border while a creepy, low voice bellowed, "THEY KEEP COMING." I couldn't stand the eerie music and the Darth Vader voice.

Mr. Miller put his baby back rib down and licked his gooey fingers. "I'll tell you something, if those illegals keep coming, there'll be nothin' left for the rest of us," he said.

I glared at them out of the side of my eyes. The term *illegals* was so mean, it always made me jerk backward whenever I heard it. I wanted to take his gooey baby back rib and stick it in his hair.

Instead, I looked around for my best friend, Lupe. She was up on the roof with her dad, watching the sunset. I waved and smiled at her, remembering the long, wonderful summer we'd had, all the late-afternoon swims in the pool and game nights in Billy Bob's room. It was just like I'd written about in my essay for the Vermont motel contest.

"Mia!" Hank called to me from the grill. He was still in his mall security-guard uniform, having just gotten off work. The hours were long at his job, but he was hopeful that a big promotion was just around the corner, which would mean he'd have more free time. "Hand me those napkins, will ya?" Hank asked me with a smile.

I got Hank a thick stack of napkins. As he grilled the ribs, I told him what I'd heard Mr. Miller say. The hickory smoke of the ribs mixed with the frustration in my nose.

"It's those awful ads," Hank said, frowning. He brushed the ribs with his honey barbecue sauce. "They're scapegoating the immigrants for California's problems."

"*What*-goating?" I asked. I pictured a billy goat in the middle of the pool, bleating and splashing toward us.

"Scapegoating's when you blame someone else for things that go wrong, even if they had nothing to do with it," Hank explained. He adjusted his hat to block the lazy summer sun from his eyes.

"There's a word for that? I thought it was just called plain ol' mean," I said.

Hank chuckled.

As the ribs sizzled on the grill, I thought back to last year.

"Is it kind of like when we had to pay Mr. Yao for the broken washing machine?" I asked Hank, wincing a little at the memory. It had been a long, hard year, and sometimes I still got goose bumps when I thought about the many, many things Mr. Yao docked our salary for.

"Exactly," Hank said, tapping the meat with his barbecue fork. "Put it this way: Governor Wilson has a very large broken washing machine, called the California economy, and now he needs someone to blame."

My mother waved at me from the other side of the pool. She and my dad were standing next to their friends, Uncle Zhang and

Auntie Ling. I waved back and called, "Be right there!" Then I turned to Hank and asked, "But why immigrants?"

He put his barbecue prong down and thought for a minute. Finally, he said, "Because it's easy to blame those in a weak spot."

As Hank returned to his barbecue, I thought about Lupe's two roller coasters saying. It was bad enough to be stuck on the poor one without other people trying to make the ride even longer and *more* shaky. I stared into the blurry heat above the grill, my heart thumping.

. . .

After all the guests left later that night, I found Lupe sitting on the stairs in the back of the motel. I took a seat next to her.

"Can you believe it's already the middle of August?" Lupe asked, leaning her head against my shoulder and smiling in the dreamy, sticky heat. We looked up at the bright full moon and listened to the fireworks going off at Disneyland, five miles away. We couldn't see them, but we could hear them every night. "I wish the summer would never end."

"Me too," I said. Lupe offered me a watermelon wedge from her paper plate, and I bit into it, the sweetness of the watermelon lingering on my tongue.

As I gazed up at the stars, I thought about how amazing this was. To be able to sit here and listen to the fireworks and not have to worry that Mr. Yao might drive over and yell at us to get back to work. Now instead of threats and harassment, we had a new credit card reader, a new vending machine, How to Navigate America classes for new immigrants on Wednesdays, hosted by Mrs. T and

Mrs. Q, and Lucky Penny search nights on Tuesdays, organized by my dad.

My parents were no longer walking zombies, thanks to a sign up at the front office that Lupe and I made that said, *Catching some z's. Please come back in the morning! The front desk is open from 6 a.m. to 11 p.m.*

The first night my parents put up that sign, they kept waking up at night, hearing customers in their heads. It was as though people were checking in between their right ear and their left ear. It took a week for them to accept that they were no longer nocturnal, but finally they started sleeping soundly all night long.

Lupe turned to me and asked, "We're still going to do this when school starts, right? Check people in together?"

"Are you kidding?" I asked. "Of course!" I loved working at the front desk with my best friend. *Best friend.* I rolled the words around in my mouth. They were words I never got to say before, having moved to four different schools for six different grades. Now I got to say them whenever I wanted!

"Oh, I almost forgot," Lupe said, pulling a piece of paper from her pocket and handing it to me. "My dad had to go home early, but he said to give you guys this."

I opened the note. The words *Channel 624* and *Channel 249* were scribbled inside.

"They're the Chinese news channels," she said. "He finally managed to get them to work so your parents can watch the Chinese news!"

I grinned. "They'll be so excited! Tell him thanks!"

Lupe took her watermelon rind, held it up to her mouth, and beamed a gigantic green smile at me.

One of the guest room doors opened, and the sound of the *Channel 5 Evening News* spilled into the night. The words *illegal immigration* thundered from the room. I jerked back again. I never used to hear that term before. Now I heard it five times a day.

"Have you seen the ads on TV?" I turned to Lupe and asked.

Lupe's watermelon smile disappeared. She put her wedge down and asked, "What ads?" like she didn't know what I was talking about. Which was impossible. You'd have to be a Martian not to have seen them all summer.

"Don't worry, he's not going to win," I told her gently. I thought about telling her what Hank said about the goat named Scape.

Lupe wrapped her arms tightly around her knees and hunched into a ball. "So, you ready for school to start tomorrow?" she asked, changing the subject. "I hope we're in the same class again this year."

"Me too!"

"Hope we're not in the same class as Jason Yao," she added, making a face.

I laughed. "He's not that bad." Actually, I'd thought about Jason a few times this summer. I hadn't heard from him. I bet he went on a long fancy vacation with his parents, staying at one of those hotels with the huge breakfast buffets. I wished we could have one at the Calivista. I wondered if he thought about us as he munched on his chocolate croissants. I'd kind of hoped he'd call me. Then I could tell him how well we were doing.

There were a couple of days that summer when we had rented

out every single room. That had never happened before. We even got to light up the *No Vacancy* sign! My dad let me flick the switch. As I lit the sign, I fantasized about Mr. Yao driving past, his face fuming with regret.

"Jason *is* that bad," Lupe insisted. Her face turned all red and I stared at her, half amused.

"He's changed a lot," I reminded her. "He was the one who helped us negotiate with Mr. Yao for the motel, remember?"

Still, Lupe shook her head. "People don't change."

I studied her, her hands squeezed tight into little fists around her knees, as Hank came running over.

"Mia! Lupe! Come quick! You guys gotta see this! We're on TV!"

CHAPTER 2

We all gathered around the small TV in the manager's quarters. Hank turned the volume all the way up while Lupe, the weeklies, my parents, and I sat cross-legged on the floor. Everyone leaned toward the screen.

There, on the evening news, was a man standing directly across the street from the Calivista, holding up a small dog. The dog had been found right here on Coast Boulevard, hiding under a parked car. As the owner tearfully explained how thrilled he was to have his dog back after three months of agonizing over where he was, we all stared at the giant *Calivista Motel* sign just to the left of his head.

"This is free advertising!" Fred shouted. We all jumped up and shook hands, congratulating one another on our amazing luck. My mom poured everyone cups of jasmine tea as my dad hopped on the phone and started calling his immigrant friends and the paper investors to tell them the good news.

Billy Bob pointed at the TV. "How much do you think a spot like that would have cost?"

Fred whistled. "Thousands of dollars, I'd say!" His belly shook as he laughed.

Mrs. T flipped to Channel 4 and everyone gasped. We were on

Channel 4 too! Lupe and I jumped up and down and started doing our happy dance.

Hank held up his index finger. "I have an idea!" he exclaimed. He looked to my parents. "Where's the ladder? I need to add some words to our sign!"

My parents took Hank to the back alley behind the pool, where they kept the ladder that José used to fix the cable up on the roof. Fred and Billy Bob helped Hank move it in front of the towering Calivista sign. As Hank grabbed the letters to the new words he wanted to put up, we all looked up at the sign.

"You're not thinking of climbing all the way up there, are you?" Mrs. T asked Hank. The sign was easily twenty feet tall. "It's much too high!"

"Don't do it, Hank!" I seconded. What if he fell? We still didn't have health insurance. We'd tried to buy some as a small business, but the only plan that was affordable had a minimum requirement of six full-time employees. The insurance company said investors didn't count.

But Hank was already halfway up the ladder, the letters gripped in one hand. As he added the new words to the sign, we all held our breath. It wasn't until he was safely back down that we read the message.

There, under the words *CALIVISTA MOTEL, $20/NIGHT*, and *5 MILES FROM DISNEYLAND*, were four words that made my heart swell with pride: *AS SEEN ON TV*.

Leave it to Hank to think up the perfect way to take advantage of our fifteen minutes of fame!

* * *

I rubbed my eyes the next morning, awoken by the sound of honking horns on the boulevard. Peeking out the window, I could see customers already lined up at the front office, ready to check in.

"Mom! Dad! Wake up!" I yelled, jumping out of bed.

My parents and I changed out of our pajamas and quickly got to work, checking people in and handling requests for wake-up calls and late checkouts. The new sign was bringing people in faster than you could say *Calivista*!

Hank stopped to say good morning as he was getting ready for his day, and when he saw how busy we were, he immediately stepped behind the front desk. Hank was a natural checker-iner. He loved talking to the customers, and they loved talking to him. Everyone wanted to know how we were on TV, and as soon as he told them the story of Cody the puppy being found just across the street, the customers all *awww*ed.

I glanced down hesitantly at my backpack lying beside the front desk, not quite ready to leave. It was all packed up for my first day of sixth grade.

"Go, Mia," my dad said. "We've got it covered."

"But—"

"We'll be fine here. You're going to be late for school," Hank said, looking at the clock. It was nearly 8:00. My fingers lingered on the row of keys hanging next to the stack of registration forms. We were running low on the forms. Expertly, Hank tore open a box of fresh new ones and set them on the table.

I picked up my backpack. "Okay," I said. My mom handed me a custard bun for breakfast. I stopped by the kitchen and when she wasn't looking, swapped it for a granola bar. At the door, I stopped and turned back. "Wait, what about your job at the mall?" I asked Hank.

"Don't worry about it." He waved me off. "I'll just take one of my vacation days. I still have a bunch!"

. . .

I ate my granola bar as I walked the familiar two blocks down Meadow Lane to my school. It was a Great Value bar, not like the Quaker Chewy ones the other kids ate at school. My dad said it didn't matter, they were all the same inside. He didn't eat any granola bars himself, preferring the Bin Bin rice crackers from the Chinese grocery store. But I liked the granola bars better.

As I tossed back the rest of my breakfast, a white Mercedes came roaring behind me, screeching to a stop. I turned around to see Jason and his mom pulling up to me, and I quickly scrunched up the wrapper and stuck it in my pocket. Mrs. Yao waved from behind the wheel, her enormous diamond ring catching in the light.

"Get in," Jason said, jumping out of the car. "We'll give you a ride."

He looked different, taller and with stiffer hair. Had he gelled it? His eyes smiled back at me while he waited. I hesitated for a second — what would Lupe say if she saw me arriving at school in Jason's car? But it was 102 degrees outside, and I could feel the car's air conditioning beckoning me from the sidewalk. I climbed inside and sank into the soft leather seat.

"How was your summer?" Jason asked me as his mother drove.

I had been practicing what to say when I saw him again, a

casual but impressive story complete with sales figures: We managed to double our occupancy rates, the number of repeat customers went up by 50 percent, *and* we helped twenty-five immigrants, providing them free rooms and meals to help them get on their feet.

But in my excitement and haste, all that came out was, "Good." I quickly added, "How about you? Did you go anywhere?"

I waited for the itinerary of no fewer than three continents, but Jason shook his head and said, "Nah."

I lifted my eyes from the automatic window controls, surprised. "You didn't go anywhere?"

"Yeah, I just stayed home," he said.

His mom called from the front, "We traveled way too much last summer, didn't we, sweetie?"

Jason gazed out the window and didn't say anything. As we pulled up at school, I spotted Lupe in her mom's car and waved to Mrs. Garcia. Mrs. Garcia had on a bright red headband and smiled at me as she waved back. A few times this summer, she'd come along with her husband to the motel. She always brought over great big bowls of freshly made guacamole and chips, and we'd all dive in. A few times, she even pitched in and helped my parents clean the rooms when it was a full house. Lupe's eyes darted from me to Mrs. Yao to Jason, and she raised her drawing pad to her face like a shield.

I thanked Mrs. Yao for the ride and got out of the car, running over to Lupe to tell her about all the new customers this morning.

"That's amazing!" she squealed, peeking over at Mrs. Yao. "The sign must have worked!"

"What sign?" Jason asked, walking over to us.

Quickly, I told Jason about being on TV.

"Really?" he asked. "What channel? I can't believe I missed it." Then with a groan, he added, "All I did was watch TV this summer."

Lupe's face turned red. The bell rang, and she grabbed my hand and pulled me away from Jason, toward the classrooms.

The walls of Dale Elementary School were adorned with hand-drawn blue-and-gold *WELCOME BACK* posters. Unlike last year, the walls were not freshly painted, but they still looked warm and inviting. As we walked down the halls, the younger kids scattered out of our way, gazing at us in awe. I smiled, remembering what it was like to be a fourth grader, looking up at a sixth grader. They seemed as powerful as the sun, like if you stared at one too long, you might go blind. I couldn't believe I was now a sun.

Lupe and I walked arm in arm to the front office, where we learned that we were in the same class again — Mrs. Welch's class! Jason was so bummed he wasn't in Mrs. Welch's class too, he threw his backpack down on the floor in a fit of frustration, and as if that wasn't enough, he stomped on it.

Lupe started tugging my arm away from Jason and out of the office, but I resisted her pull. I wasn't ready to go to class just yet.

"Hey, it's going to be okay," I said gently to Jason.

Jason turned to the receptionist. "Can I switch classes? Please? I want to be in Mrs. Welch's class too!"

The receptionist shook her head. "Sorry, I'm afraid not. All the classroom assignments are final."

Jason stuck out his lower lip.

Lupe tapped my arm again, holding the door open with her foot. "He'll be fine," she insisted.

I glanced at Jason, who looked far from fine. He was staring at the receptionist the way some of our customers did whenever we told them we were all out of double beds.

Slowly, I walked over and put a hand on his back. "Hey, we'll still see each other at recess," I offered. Jason hung his head, nodding slightly.

CHAPTER 3

Ten minutes later, Lupe and I found our new classroom way in the back of the school, except it wasn't a classroom, it was an air-conditioned trailer! Hesitantly, Lupe and I opened the door to the trailer, thinking there must be some kind of mistake. But a thin white woman gestured for us to come in, so we did.

"I'm Mrs. Welch," the woman said. "Please take a seat." She pointed to the desks, where rows of similarly confused-looking students sat. I recognized Bethany Brett, the girl who had made fun of my math last year. Bethany rolled her eyes at me. Clearly, she was thrilled to see me too. I walked over to the two empty desks way on the other side of the room, far, far away from Bethany. As Lupe and I set our things down, Mrs. Welch made an *uh-uh* sound.

"Sorry, but you can't sit with your friends," Mrs. Welch said, shaking her head. She pointed at Lupe and motioned for her to take the seat next to Bethany's instead. "Sit here."

As Lupe reluctantly moved her stuff over to the other side of the room, I sat at my desk, my jaw clenching in frustration.

"Good morning, class." Mrs. Welch had a tight brown bun on her head, like her hair had been pulled back with a vacuum cleaner. Her cheekbones were razor sharp, and she forced her paper-thin lips into a stiff smile as she scanned the room.

"Good morning, Mrs. Welch," we replied.

"You're probably wondering why we're in a trailer," she said. I looked around the room. Several kids were nodding. One was asleep. And another kid was scratching his head and smelling his fingers.

"Well, the classroom we were supposed to be in had a little water damage," Mrs. Welch explained. "We were hoping to fix it over the summer, but unfortunately, due to budget cuts . . ." Her voice trailed off.

There was another phrase we'd heard a lot this summer: *due to budget cuts*. There was a collective groan in the classroom, which Mrs. Welch cut short with a clap of her hands. "Right, then. We're not going to dwell on that. Get out your pencils. We're going to start the school year off by writing a little reflection."

I sat up very straight. *YES!* I was dying to get back to writing. The reports for the paper investors were fun, but I longed for the freedom and challenge of fiction.

"I'm sure you've all heard about the gubernatorial race," she said.

"Gubana-what?" Stuart, in the back, asked.

A few kids laughed.

"Gubernatorial!" Mrs. Welch repeated.

We all just giggled harder. Except Lupe—her head was down, and she was drawing in her sketch pad.

Mrs. Welch wrote *GUBERNATORIAL* on the board, but still we couldn't pronounce it. She finally had to ditch it and go with the word *governor* instead.

"Governor Wilson is running for reelection," she said. "One of the things he's running on is immigration. Do you guys know what *immigration* means?"

I raised my hand. "It's when someone comes to this country from another country."

Mrs. Welch frowned. "Yes, but please wait until you are called on before speaking next time," she scolded me. "This is the sixth grade. You need to follow the rules."

I felt my cheeks turn hot.

Bethany Brett raised her hand and blurted out, "I heard it cost the state of California 1.5 billion dollars just to take care of immigrants."

"That's right," Mrs. Welch said. She nodded at Bethany, pleased. "Someone's been paying attention to the news."

I couldn't believe it. Mrs. Welch had just snapped at me for not waiting to be called on before speaking, but when Bethany did it, she was all jazz hands and dancing fingers. I shook my head and stared at the glued-on "wooden" walls of our trailer classroom. Sixth grade was off to some start.

• • •

At recess, Jason walked up to me and Lupe. We were talking about Mrs. Welch.

"Can you believe that woman?" I asked Lupe. "She yelled at me in the first five minutes of class!"

"*And* she made us write about immigration," Lupe added. She mimicked Mrs. Welch's voice. "'Write your true feelings. There are no right or wrong answers.' YEAH RIGHT."

"Writing already? On the first day?" Jason shuddered. "*We* just sat around and introduced ourselves."

"For the entire morning?" I asked.

"Oh, yeah. You'd be amazed how long you can stretch that out for." Jason grinned. "At *least* a morning, sometimes even an entire day!"

I chuckled. It sounded like he was feeling better about his class.

Then he turned to me and asked, "Hey, so you want to come over to my house after school next Friday and hang out?"

I glanced over at Lupe, who was jiggling her head from side to side like a Chinese rattle drum. But I remembered the disappointment on Jason's face that morning, when he found out we weren't in the same class. "Sure . . ." I said slowly. "We're free next Friday, right, Lupe?"

She shot me a look. "I think I have to help my dad out with something," she muttered.

"How about you, Mia?" Jason asked, eagerly.

"I, uh . . ."

"Oh, c'mon, it's going to be so awesome. Wait till you see my house."

"I've been to your house," I reminded him. Last year, when we first met his dad. And his dad tricked us into working at the motel for practically free.

"Yeah, but not as . . . you know . . ." His voice trailed off.

I shook my head. "As what?"

Jason blushed.

"As a friend."

Awwww. I looked over at Lupe, who had *Excuse me while I go throw up* written on her face. But was it really so bad to be friends with him? Sure, Jason was a world-class buffoon last year, but you can't hold something against someone forever, can you?

"Okay," I said.

. . .

"How was school?" my parents asked when I walked into the motel that afternoon. My mom set down a plate of tomato and egg, my favorite, while my dad scooped a generous helping of rice for me. I smiled. Now that my parents could take breaks whenever they wanted, they could sit down with me while I had my snack. Which was more like a meal. Though I got free lunch at school, it usually wasn't enough, and my belly was rumbling by the time I got home.

"Good," I said, picking up my chopsticks. The chopsticks kept falling apart in my hands, so I ditched them for a fork. As I ate, I told my parents about my new teacher and how we'd gotten off to a rocky start—but that it would be okay, since I was going to win her over with my writing.

"That's the spirit," my mom said. She looked over to my dad, but he was too busy staring at my hand.

"You're eating *rice* with a fork?" he asked.

I blushed and quickly switched to a spoon. Was that a better utensil? Dad smiled a little. I ate the rest of my food quietly. As I cleared the plates and tossed my unused chopsticks in the sink, I wondered why it mattered so much to Dad what I used to eat with, so long as I got the food in my mouth?

CHAPTER 4

The next day at recess, Lupe brought up going over to Jason's house.

"Are you sure it's a good idea?" she asked, pushing open the door to the bathroom.

I followed her inside and went into one of the stalls. "I mean, I'm not, like, *looking forward to it*, but I'm not dreading it either," I answered truthfully. I was a tiny bit worried about bumping into Mr. Yao. But he'd probably be at work.

"So why are you going?" Lupe asked from the stall next to me. She skipped a beat and then asked, "Do you like Jason?"

Before I had a chance to reply—*No way! I don't* like *him*—a group of girls came into the bathroom talking loudly.

"My mom says she's pretty sure there are illegals in our class," said one of the girls. I peeked through the crack in the stall. It was Gloria, a girl who thankfully was not in our class.

Over in her stall, Lupe was as quiet as a church mouse.

"How can you tell them apart?" asked Gloria's friend.

"That's easy. If they speak English with an accent."

The two girls giggled.

Very quietly, I lifted my feet so that the girls couldn't see them if they looked under the stall. I shrank so small, I nearly fell into the toilet.

Despite my best efforts, *I* still spoke English with a slight accent.

Lupe and I waited until the girls left before reemerging from our stalls. When we came out, Lupe turned to me, obviously as shaken by what she heard as I was.

"Just ignore them," she said.

I kept my head down as I washed my hands. Easy for her to say. She had no accent at all.

. . .

After school on Wednesday, we hurried along Meadow Lane, eager to get back to the motel and help set up for the How to Navigate America class that Mrs. T and Mrs. Q taught every week in Mrs. T's room. Lupe and I helped translate, and sometimes I would write letters for any immigrants who needed help with various situations.

Thanks to Lupe's Spanish, we were now able to serve not only Chinese immigrants but Latino uncles and aunties too, and their kids. They learned things like how to open a bank account and how to get around on public transportation. My mom taught their children math in another room. It was her favorite night of the week.

Hank was in the front office when we got back. "You won't believe it! Ever since that TV spot, your dad says we've been getting twice the business," he announced, gesturing for us to come look at the cash register. Lupe and I put our backpacks down and ducked below the front desk divider. Our eyes widened at the heaps of cash.

"That's the power of advertising!" Hank beamed and hopped

off the stool. "You know what I'm going to do? I'm going to go down to the paper during my lunch hour next week to see how much it costs to run a real ad."

My dad came running in from the kitchen, just behind the front office, looking alarmed. "How much is that going to cost?"

"Relax, buddy." Hank put a hand on my dad's shoulder as he grabbed his room key. "Print ads aren't as expensive as TV ads."

"But why do we have to do *any* ads?" Dad asked.

I remembered something else Lupe had told me about America: Sometimes you gotta pay to play. I grinned — we were in the big leagues now. This was us playing. I reached for my dad's hand and led him outside, pointing up at the *AS SEEN ON TV* sign. "Have faith, Dad."

After Hank left, my mom came into the manager's quarters. She was hunched over with one hand on her back and the other hand on her knee. "I'm so sore from cleaning," she said, cringing as she sank onto her bed in the living room. I sighed, wishing we had enough money for her to see a chiropractor for her back. Cleaning was starting to take a toll on her.

"Here, Mom," I said, walking over to her and putting my hand to her shoulder. "Let me massage your muscles."

My mother lay down on her bed and cooed, "Oh, you sweet thing," as I massaged her.

"Hold on," I said. I'd seen this thing on TV where if you massaged someone with coconut oil, it felt good. We didn't have any coconut oil — that was way too pricey — but we had sesame oil. I got it from the kitchen and slathered it on my mom's arm.

"That feels sooo good!" Mom said. "My muscles are like rubber bands that have hardened and become sticks!"

"Well, if you're a stick, I'm a tree trunk," my dad chuckled, sitting down beside her. He held out his hand. "Put some of that here, will ya?"

I squeezed a few drops of sesame oil on his hand and my dad rubbed his neck with it.

"That smells great," he said, closing his eyes and inhaling the nutty aroma. "Now all you need is to crack an egg, throw some spring onions on me, and you'll have yourself a delicious *jianbing*." He cackled.

I furrowed my eyebrows. "What's *jianbing*?"

"*Jianbing?* You don't remember *jianbingguozi*?" He stopped massaging his neck and looked at me, shocked. "It's a Chinese breakfast. We used to buy it on the streets in Beijing. How can you not remember?"

I shook my head, trying for the life of me to remember, but I just couldn't.

My dad sighed. I could tell he was disappointed I had forgotten yet another remnant of the old country. "I hope you're not becoming a banana," he joked. A banana was what Chinese people called a kid who has gotten too Americanized — yellow on the outside and white on the inside. If it came from anyone else, I'd be super offended, but I knew my parents were just kidding. Still, it hurt a little, like a tiny mosquito bite.

"Oh, stop, she's not a banana," my mom piped up from the bed. "Now put some more of that stuff on me."

. . .

As my mom wiped the sesame oil off her sore arms and neck and got ready for her math class, Lupe and I went over to Mrs. T's room. Today, there were five Latino and three Chinese uncles and aunties there. They beamed and quickly gestured for me to come over and help them write letters to various people and departments — the phone company, the bank, etc. I took a seat at my special desk Mrs. T set up for me, feeling very official.

As Lupe chatted with the Latino uncles and aunties, my mom came over to collect their kids. The boys and girls, ages five, seven, and ten, sniffed the air — my mom smelled of sesame oil and Lysol, which must have been a very peculiar smell to them. To me, it smelled like home.

"C'mon, kids," she said. As they moved to the room next door I heard her ask, "Who's ready to learn some math today?"

In our room, Mrs. Q passed out papers and pens. Lupe was talking animatedly with one of the aunties in Spanish.

"They said they're from Jalisco. They've just crossed over," Lupe translated, then paused. "They tried crossing over from San Diego, but there were too many Border Patrol officers. So they had to go through Arizona."

My mouth formed an O. Though we'd been talking about it at school and I'd heard about illegal immigration all summer on TV, this was the first time I'd seen it up close. I knew some of my parents' friends knew Chinese immigrants who had overstayed their visas, but I hadn't yet met them. The uncles and aunties from Jalisco looked nothing like the grainy figures in the TV ads. One of them took an orange from his pocket and kindly offered it to me and Lupe. His hands were dry and cracked, even drier than my mom's.

"They want to know if you can write a letter to the Border Patrol. An anonymous letter," Lupe translated. "Asking them to look for their friend. They walked for days in the scorching Sonoran desert. And it got so hot that unfortunately, their friend . . ." She stopped translating and wiped a tear from her cheek.

"Their friend what?" I asked, the ink from my pen pooling on my forefinger and thumb.

Lupe put a hand over her mouth and shook her head. Mrs. Q and Mrs. T stepped in. "I'll write it," Mrs. T volunteered. With that, she turned to the immigrants and in her gentlest, kindest teacher voice introduced herself. "I'm Mrs. T. . . ."

"And I'm Mrs. Q," Mrs. Q chimed in. "And today we're going to talk about the DMV."

Later, after class, I found Lupe lingering in the back of my mom's math class.

"Are you okay?" I asked her.

Lupe nodded. I asked her if she was sad because of what the Mexican auntie and uncle said, and she nodded without looking up. I put a hand on her back. In the pale lamplight, I thought about my own journey to America and how different it was compared to walking across the scorching desert. Still, it was scary and full of uncertainty.

"I'm so sorry about their friend," I said to Lupe. I'd heard about border-crossing tragedies on the news, but lately I really wondered whether it was worth it, especially considering the way people were treated once they got here. "And those girls in the bathroom . . ."

"They were pretty bad." Lupe agreed. Then she rubbed her eyes and turned to me, sitting up as straight as she could. "But people are going to think what they're going to think. You just have to ignore them and keep doing your thing."

I nodded. "I will if you will."

CHAPTER 5

On Saturday my mom woke me up bright and early. She sat down on my bed with a pair of scissors in one hand and a bowl in the other.

"Time for a haircut, Mia!"

I groaned. "Does it have to be today?"

"C'mon, you want to look extra good when we go out with all your dad's friends tonight, don't you?"

I glanced hesitantly at the bowl. At the start of every school year, my parents would put a bowl over my head and cut the hair around it. They considered this to be basically the same as a professional haircut. I considered it the same as getting sheared — I always came out looking like an alpaca, with bits of hair sticking out all over the place.

"Please, this year, can I go to a real barber?" I sat up and begged.

Mom looked all offended. "I *am* a real barber," she insisted, snipping the air with her scissors as if to demonstrate.

My dad walked in, nodding. "Going to a real barber is too wasteful," he said. He got his own bowl haircut every other month. "And besides, it'll only take ten minutes."

I walked over to the mirror and gazed at my head of wild,

untamed hair. Sure, it looked a bit like a mop, but did she have to chop it all off and make me look like a mushroom again?

"Can we just skip this year?" I asked.

My mom shook her head. "Long hair wastes shampoo," she said.

"I'll only wash my roots! And I'll keep it up in a ponytail, so it doesn't get in my face," I promised.

My mom put a finger to her chin and studied my face as though it were a flower arrangement. Finally, she sighed.

"Fine, we'll just do the bangs."

YES!

I took the bowl from her and put it over my forehead. "*Just* my bangs!"

As my mom put her scissors to my hair, I closed my eyes, hoping I wouldn't come out looking like a chopped salad.

• • •

Later that night, I was feeling my newly cropped bangs with my fingers as we all piled into the car to go out to dinner with my dad's buddies, the immigrant investors. My dad had been looking forward to this dinner all week, and Hank had volunteered to man the front desk so we could all go. We were meeting at Buffet Paradise, an all-you-can-eat restaurant.

"Remember, when we get there, don't fill up on bread or rice," my dad advised from the driver's seat. When it came to buffets, my dad had more strategy than an army general. "Go straight for the crab legs and shrimp!"

"Or the ribs!" my mom added.

I rubbed my hands together. We hadn't eaten all day in preparation for the big meal.

When we arrived, a bunch of my dad's friends were already there, helping themselves to the slow-roasted beef tips, skipping the mashed potatoes. Like us, they had dressed strategically, in loose pants and big shirts.

My dad took a seat at the head of the table and started handing out checks to all his friends, their share of the motel profits that month. Dad was always enormously proud when he was handing out checks to his friends, his face shining like a steamed bun. And he should be. So many of them had put their hard-earned money into the Calivista and were counting on their portion of the profits.

"You know what we're going to do with this money?" Auntie Ling asked. "We're going to put it toward a second car!"

"Ooooooh!" My mom scooted over closer to Auntie Ling to get all the details—what make and model, what color. I knew she'd been itching to get one too, but my dad said it was too expensive.

Uncle Zhang, who was now parking cars over in Burbank, said in between bites, "With my cut, I'm going to study for a better job!"

My dad looked up from his crab leg. "What are you thinking of studying?" he asked.

"I was gonna try to take the electrical technician exam." Like my mom, Uncle Zhang was an engineer back in China. I smiled as he told us his plans. He had come such a long way from being trapped in the basement of his employer's house last year, working day and night. He pointed a rib at my mom.

"Ying, you should do it too!" Uncle Zhang exclaimed. "We could do it together!"

My mom turned to my dad, and they shared a look. "Can't," she said with a slight shake of her head. "Too busy cleaning rooms."

All around the table, the aunties and uncles put down their food and held up their drinks. "And we appreciate it," they said, toasting my parents. My parents smiled.

As everyone got up to get more food, I thought about my mom's answer. Was she not happy cleaning rooms? Did she want to do something else instead? But we finally owned the motel, and business was going so well!

When I looked up, the adults were back with their third plates and talking about Proposition 187, the law that Governor Wilson wanted to pass. That's what all the ads were for. If it passed, Prop 187 would kick undocumented children out of California schools, making it illegal for them to get an education or use public services like hospitals.

"Such a shame. My cousin's kid is going to be affected," Auntie Ling said. "They just got here from Changsha."

"I myself almost became undocumented," Uncle Zhang said, shaking his head. "If it weren't for Mia, I wouldn't have gotten my passport back from my employer on time to renew my visa." He reached out and patted my hand. I smiled.

"But isn't the legislation mostly targeting Mexicans?" Uncle Fung asked.

"We immigrants are all in the same boat," my dad reminded his friends. "Don't let them divide and conquer us. If this law passes, it's bad for all of us."

The aunties and uncles all nodded at my dad's words as they ate. When at last I could feel my pants about to pop, my dad got up and settled the bill before any of his friends could protest. I looked to my mom, whose eyes were moving around the table, her lips silently counting as she did the math of how much the meal cost. My dad didn't need to do the math. Pride filled me up as my dad paid, even more than the crab legs did.

CHAPTER 6

On the way home, my mother sat next to me in the back of the car and asked my dad how much the bill was.

"Don't worry about it," he said, batting away her concern with a hand. "It was good to see everyone, wasn't it?"

"Yes, but I don't know why you always have to *pay* for everyone."

"Of course we have to pay," Dad said. "We're Chinese, that's what we do." He glanced at my mom in the rearview mirror. "What, did you want us to *split* it?" He uttered the word *split* like it was a curse word.

"No, but there are things I'd like to be able to buy for *us*."

"Like what?"

My mom shrugged. "Like a second car?"

"A second car? But we're always at the motel!" He turned around and looked at my mom. "Do you have any idea how much a second car costs?"

"We could buy it on a credit card!" I offered. Now that we had a card machine, I got to see for myself the magic of these little cards. All you had to do is swipe, sign, and boom. All paid!

My mom's eyes lit up. "That's a great idea! We should get a credit card!"

"No, no, no, that's a terrible idea," Dad vetoed. "We're not spending money before we have it. That's such an American thing to do."

"No, but we *will* pay for twenty people's dinner," my mom muttered under her breath.

The topic of credit cards was put on hold for the rest of the car ride. When we got back to the motel, my parents thanked Hank for covering the desk.

"Hey, Hank, what do you think of credit cards?" my mom asked.

Hank hopped off the stool and slapped a hand on our credit card machine. "Did you know you get a ton of miles on those things?"

"What are miles?" I asked Hank.

Hank explained that most credit cards reward you for using them to buy stuff by giving you free airplane miles, so you can fly to places and get a vacation for free. I poked my dad. Free vacation. I liked the sound of that.

"Yeah, but only if you spend enough money, which we're not going to," my dad replied.

"You never know. I'm applying for one myself," Hank informed us. He tilted his head and made a dreamy face. "Can you see me frolicking around the Bahamas?"

I giggled. I could *totally* see that.

. . .

Later, I found my mom in the laundry room, except she wasn't doing any laundry or folding towels. She was bent over on the small stool filling out a bunch of papers.

"Mom, why are you doing that in here?" The laundry room was

so damp and sweaty, you could start growing bean sprouts on your nose if you stayed in there too long.

My mom jerked up from the papers, surprised and slightly embarrassed. "You scared me."

I looked down at the papers. They were math worksheets for her students, hand drawn and hand copied. There was even a line where she had written *Name:_____* on the top, like a real teacher. I smiled. Then I noticed another piece of paper beside the stack of math papers. Across the top it read *APPLICATION FOR CREDIT CARD.*

"Hank had an extra copy," my mom explained. "It can't hurt to apply, right?"

"Wow," I said, impressed. "But what about Dad and not spending money we don't have?"

My mom gave me a look. "You think with your mom's eye for numbers, we're gonna get too carried away?" she asked with a wink.

I smiled again. Fair enough. I pointed at all her math worksheets and asked her how that was going.

"Good," she said. "Some of the students are getting it. You know who's *really* good at math? Lupe."

"Really?" I asked. I always figured Lupe to be more of an art person. She drew such breathtaking landscapes.

My mom nodded. "But I need to buy some calculators and a real whiteboard if I'm going to teach more complicated stuff," she said. She glanced down at her credit card application and sighed. "I wish I had fewer rooms to clean and more time to do math." Her eyes shifted to the mountain of dirty towels next to her. Every day, there was a new tower.

"Would you want to go for your engineering exam or a technician's exam like Uncle Zhang?" I asked, thinking about what she'd said at dinner.

My mom thought long and hard. "No," she finally decided. "Because then I wouldn't be able to see you all the time."

I smiled at the gray tile floor. I wasn't sure if she really meant that or if she was just saying that to make me (and her) feel better. But either way, I felt relieved.

Softly, I told my mom about what the girls in the bathroom said yesterday.

"And what do you think it means to have an accent?" my mom asked.

"I don't know," I muttered. *Something I have now, but if I work really, really hard, maybe someday I'll get rid of it?*

My mom put a hand over my knee. "Want to know what I think?"

I met her eyes hesitantly, half afraid she'd come up with another devastating transportation analogy. Instead she said, "I think an accent is like your very own unique signature of all the places you've been. Like stamps in a passport. It has nothing to do with where you're going."

I smiled at her in surprise. "Thanks, Mom."

She smiled too. "Speaking of signatures," she said, lifting her pen.

And that night, under the hot, roaring laundry machines, my mom signed her very first credit card application.

CHAPTER 7

On Sunday, the governor's race was in the news again and at school the next day, Mrs. Welch was back at it, talking about Proposition 187. She had a small *Wilson for Governor* button on the lapel of her blazer, and she was petting it fondly, like it was a furry cat.

"Why do they call it the Save Our State law?" Mrs. Welch asked.

This time, I raised my hand.

When she finally called on me, I said, "Because it's goatscaping," and sat up at my desk, proud to have said such a big word. Except I got it wrong.

"*Scape*goating," Mrs. Welch corrected.

A few kids in the back row snickered.

I looked over at Lupe, who mouthed *ignore them*. But as Mrs. Welch continued talking about Prop 187, I could tell Lupe was having a hard time taking her own advice too.

"It's a matter of math, folks," Mrs. Welch said. She started jotting down numbers. "There are four hundred thousand illegal immigrant children in our schools, and it costs us 1.5 billion dollars a year." She recited the lines from the ad like a parrot.

I shook my head. "But education is a basic human right—" I blurted out.

Mrs. Welch snapped, "How many times have I asked you to raise your hand first, wait to be called on, and then speak?"

I mumbled sorry, then raised my hand.

"What is it?" Mrs. Welch asked.

"How would you even know if a child is an 'illegal' immigrant?" I asked her.

"I think it's pretty obvious."

"Based on what?" I asked. My face got hot. "Their race?" My classmates' heads yo-yoed back and forth from me and Mrs. Welch like it was a tennis match. Lupe kept shaking her head at me, like *Just drop it!* But I couldn't. "See, that's why Prop 187 is racist."

Mrs. Welch stopped stroking her button and pointed her finger at me. "Race has nothing to do with it," she insisted. "Race isn't even real!"

Oh my God, I wanted to break a broom! I glanced over at Lupe but her head was crouched so low at her desk, her face was practically the same height as her pencil case. For the next forty-five minutes, as Mrs. Welch proceeded to explain that because race is not a biological fact, racism is not real, I sat stock-still at my desk.

When the lunch bell finally rang, I walked numbly to the cafeteria and barely noticed when Jason ran up, excited.

"My mom's going to pick us up after school on Friday," he said. "We can hang out and have dinner at my house!"

I put my free school pizza down. "I don't know about dinner. . . ." I said. The thought of dining with Mr. Yao was about as appealing as licking the inside of a toilet bowl.

I guess Jason could tell what I was thinking, because he said, "Oh, c'mon, my dad's not even going to be there. He's been working a lot lately." When I still didn't say anything, he added quickly, "Fine, you don't have to stay for dinner. But I'm going to prepare it anyway."

"You mean your housekeeper's going to prepare it," Lupe corrected.

"No. *I'm* going to prepare it." Jason crossed his arms and looked at Lupe matter-of-factly. "I'm a really good cook now."

"Oh, really," Lupe said, like she didn't believe him.

Jason nodded.

"Since when?" Lupe raised an eyebrow.

"Since the last time you knew anything about me," Jason fired back. I burst out laughing, then stopped when I saw the look on Lupe's face. *I* thought it was pretty funny. Lupe? Not so much.

. . .

After school, Lupe and I walked back to the motel, talking about Mrs. Welch and kicking rocks with our feet.

"Maybe we should do something," I said to her. "With all this 187 stuff, we can't be the only kids feeling bad."

"Like what?"

"I don't know." I shrugged. "Like start a club at school or something. Kids against 187."

Lupe stopped walking. "You want to start a club against 187 at school? You know what people will think?"

That we're brave? That we care? I thought, but I didn't have a chance to say it because Lupe answered her own question.

"That we're illegal."

Oh.

Lupe put a hand on my shoulder. "Look, I know it sucks. But

things are going to get better. This ridiculous bill is not going to pass. In three months, this will all blow over and everything's going to go back to normal."

I looked into Lupe's sure, confident eyes and hoped she was right.

Just as we got back to the motel, Hank's car pulled into the lot.

"I went down to the paper during my lunch break to talk about placing an ad," Hank said, getting out of the car.

"So how'd it go? Did you put in the ad?" I asked. He shook his head as my parents and the weeklies all came over.

"What happened? Was it too expensive?" my mom asked.

"No," Hank said. "It was about one hundred dollars a week for a small color ad right in the Metro section."

"That's not too bad. That's five customers," Lupe said.

Hank had a forlorn look on his face. "Yeah, but they didn't want to sell it to me. They said it wasn't just about the initial payment. It's about my ability to pay *long term*."

Billy Bob put his hands on his hips. "This is outrageous! Fred and I will march right back down there with you and straighten this out!" They grabbed their keys from their pockets and put their sunglasses on.

"You'd better go down without me," Hank said, sighing.

"No," Mom said firmly. "We will not advertise in a newspaper that discriminates against people based on the color of their skin."

She looked into Hank's eyes.

"We will find another newspaper," she decided.

CHAPTER 8

Hank found me by the pool later that day. I was sitting on the edge, my feet dangling in the water.

"Why the long face?" he asked me.

I kicked the water, thinking about how I said *scapegoating* wrong in class and how the paper turned him down. It was so unfair!

Hank rolled up his pants and sat down next to me, putting his feet in the water too.

"I'm mad at the paper," I confessed, making a face. "And I'm mad at my teacher. She corrected me in front of the other kids, and they all laughed."

"I'm sorry." Hank peered down at the water, his shoulders slumped forward, and traced his fingers along the surface. "If it makes you feel any better, I've been having a tough time at my job too," he said.

I sat up straighter.

"Remember the Head of Security position?" Hank turned to me. I nodded, peering at him hopefully. "They picked this other guy," he said with a frown.

"What!" I kicked the water hard with my feet, and it splashed a little on both of us. How could they? Hank was the best security guard they had. He always got to work early and helped out on the weekends if they needed him. "Did they say why?" I asked.

"They said I took too many vacation days," he said, shaking his head. "That I wasn't serious enough about my career." He dried his wet hand on his T-shirt. "Even though the other guy took the same number of vacation days."

Unbelievable. I could count on one hand the number of vacation days Hank took — and they were never to go on *actual vacation*. They were always to help out at the motel.

Hank sighed. "Ah, it's probably for the best," he said. "I don't even like that place that much. You know, ever since the Pete Wilson ads came out, my supervisor has been making really mean comments about our Mexican customers. I should just quit and try to find another job."

That's when it hit me, like a splash of cold pool water!

"Hey, why don't you work here?" I asked.

Hank chuckled, like it was a joke.

I clapped my wet hands together. "I'm serious!" I said. "The motel is getting so busy, and my parents are always cleaning. We need another manager for when Lupe and I are at school."

"It *would* be nice not to have to drive to work every day," Hank said with a dreamy smile, kicking the water with his feet.

"It would be *amazing*! All the customers love you! Plus, you have so many great ideas, like putting the *AS SEEN ON TV* sign up!"

Hank put a hand to his chin. "I do have a lot of ideas!" he chuckled.

"It's settled, then," I said, jumping to my feet and reaching out a hand to pull Hank up. After Hank and I dried ourselves off, we ran out the back to tell my parents the good news.

"That's wonderful!" my mom exclaimed.

"Hey, you know what that means? We can finally get our medical insurance! We'll have six employees!" my dad said. "Us, Mia, Lupe and her dad, and Hank—that makes six!" My dad went straight to the phone to call the insurance broker.

"First thing tomorrow, I'm going to get myself a new shirt and some nice trousers. Look like a real manager!" Hank announced.

"Great idea!" My mom beamed. "I'll go with you."

My dad put the phone down. "Wait a minute, why do you two need to go shopping?" he asked.

"Gotta dress for success, my friend," Hank said to my dad, putting a hand on his back.

"We'll only shop from the clearance rack," Mom added quickly.

I could tell from the lines on my dad's forehead that he wasn't wild about this idea. But it was hard not to feel excited. The Calivista was a real business now! And we'd just made our first hire!

• • •

I found my dad out by the pool later that night, gathering the leaves from the water with his net. I picked up my little leaf net that my mom bought me from the dollar store and started helping him.

He was unusually quiet.

"Are you worried about Hank's salary?" I asked, chewing my lip. I knew I probably should have checked with my parents first before hiring Hank, but I just couldn't resist. And they knew he was perfect for this job! "Don't worry," I said. "Business is booming. Just yesterday, I rented out twenty-five rooms! And

Hank will more than make up for his salary, he's *so* good with people!"

"It's not that. . . ." My dad sighed. "Sometimes I just feel a little guilty about what we have, compared to some of the other immigrants. . . ."

I thought about the aunties and uncles from Mexico who came the other day for Mrs. Q's class, the ones who had just crossed over.

"I know," I said.

My dad put down his long leaf net and sat on one of the pool chairs. I took a seat beside him, and we looked out at the sky, stained red and orange. Softly, my dad told me about a guy he'd met the other day who worked as a window washer and nearly died when their scaffolding collapsed.

"Things are hard for a lot of people." He sighed, resting his chin in his hands. "Sometimes I just get a little sad."

I nodded, understanding fully. "But Dad, that's no reason not to go forward," I pointed out. "We've got to get medical insurance."

My dad patted my hand. "You're right. And you know what else we're going to get? Some shaved ice." He held up a finger. "Uncle Zhang told me about a good spot in Monterey Park. What do you say this weekend, we go together?"

I smiled and said sure, though to be honest, I didn't really know what he was talking about. I figured shaved ice was another Chinese concoction, one I'd hopefully remember when I tasted it.

• • •

The next day at school, I told Lupe the great news about Hank and qualifying for insurance.

"Isn't that amazing? We finally have six full-time employees!" I cheered, counting off as I flew high on the swings.

But Lupe stopped swinging and dragged her feet on the sand. "You're going to have to find two more people," she said. "Me and my dad don't count."

"What do you mean?"

Lupe kept her eyes on the sand.

"Lupe, what's wrong?" I asked her, swinging into her slightly.

"Nothing. I'm okay. Just . . . give me a second." She held one shirt sleeve to her face. Was she crying? I got off my swing and knelt down in front of her. Lupe lifted her eyes and looked into mine. In the smallest of whispers, she let out, "We're illegal."

I wasn't sure if I heard her right. *Lupe?* My best friend, who knew this country better than anyone?

"I didn't want to tell you," she went on, blinking back tears. "We've been trying to get papers. We thought that maybe by investing in a motel, we could get an investment visa, but . . ." She shook her head. "The guy said we needed to have invested a *lot* more."

"What guy? And how much more?" I asked. Lupe and her family had already put in $10,000, which was more than my own parents had. More than even some of the paper investors!

"You don't want to know," she groaned. "Anyway, we can't apply for the medical insurance. We wouldn't qualify."

I dug my feet into the hot sand, shaking my head. "You don't know that. We can try—"

"We're *not* trying." Lupe put both hands on my arms and looked at me hard. "No one can know about this." There was an urgency in her voice I'd never heard before. "No one can *ever* know. Not with all the stuff going on."

Our foreheads touched, and I whispered, "Okay. I promise I won't tell anyone."

The recess bell rang and we walked back to class. For the rest of the day, I sat at my desk, my mind racing over what Lupe had said and what it meant. Because if Lupe was undocumented and the new law passed . . .

It meant she couldn't go to school anymore.

CHAPTER 9

Hank and my mom came to pick me up after school to go to the mall. They were in high spirits, chatting about Hank's new job title—Director of Marketing—and our new medical insurance plan. It had been years since any of us had been to the doctor for a real checkup. I sat quietly in the back of the car. I didn't have the heart to tell them we weren't getting the insurance. Not yet.

At the mall, Hank headed into Ross while my mom and I hit JCPenney. It was not my first time in JCPenney, but it was my first time as an actual customer. We had money to spend. We weren't just there to go to the bathroom!

As usual, my mother went up to the perfume counter and started spraying herself with the sample bottles. You were only supposed to try one or two on your wrist, but she tried them all on, squirting generously all over her whole body.

A salesclerk came rushing over to her. "Here, use these," she said, and held out little white strips of paper, like the pH strips we used to test the Calivista pool.

My mom shook her head. "No, thank you."

The salesclerk's smile was wearing thin. "But you're *supposed* to use these," she said.

Gently, I tugged on my mom's shirt.

"Fine," my mom said, taking the strips from the lady. She took a whole bunch and stuffed them in her purse, whispering to me, "I can use them later for a math game." The saleslady shook her head at us as we walked away.

We were poking around in the clothing clearance racks when we bumped into a trio of Chinese ladies.

"Will you look at this?" one of them said in Chinese. "This shirt has a lipstick stain on it."

"Pity, because it's so nice," her friend lamented. She glanced down at the tag and added, "And cheap too."

The three ladies huddled around the shirt and carefully studied it. "You can't get that out. It's silk," they decided, frowning.

My mom looked over. "Actually, you could probably get it out with some tape and talcum powder," she suggested. When it came to getting out laundry stains, my mom was a wizard. You wouldn't believe the makeup stains some of our customers left on the pillowcases. Still, they were no match for Mom's cleaning tricks.

The three Chinese ladies turned to my mom and gawked. "Tape?" they asked.

She nodded. "Transparent tape. Lay it over the stain, smooth it down, then quickly rip it off." She glanced quickly at me. *Should we tell them?* Her eyes twinkled. "We . . . uh . . . we own a motel."

The three ladies raised their eyebrows, impressed.

"I'm Zhou Tai Tai," one of them said, using the Chinese words for *Mrs.* She extended a hand. She had long, slender fingers adorned with various rings, unlike my mom's dry, bare ones.

"I'm Tang Tai Tai," my mom introduced herself in Chinese. "This is my daughter, Mia."

"Hi," I said.

That afternoon, Zhou Tai Tai, Fang Tai Tai, Li Tai Tai, and my mom searched through the clearance section with the intensity of hunters on a safari. They spoke in Mandarin to one another, but every time one of them spotted something really nice, they would exclaim in English, "Look at!" And the others would immediately come running over. After they searched through every last thing on sale, Mrs. Zhou and Mrs. Fang moved over to the regularly priced items section, and I looked nervously over at my mom. The regularly priced items section was a serious no-no, a high-stakes poker table you can walk by — but you do *not* sit down.

Well, my mother sat down. And the first thing she picked up was so beautiful that all the other Chinese ladies flocked around her. It was a deep red satin dress that went all the way to the floor. As the ladies oohed and aahed over how gorgeous it was and how nice it would go with a pair of heels and an evening clutch, none of which my mom had, I reached for the price tag. My fingers froze. It was $187.99!

"You should try that on!" Mrs. Zhou encouraged my mom.

"You think so?" she asked.

I yanked on her arm. "Mom, no," I whispered. I looked around for Hank. Anybody! Help! But my mother escaped with it into the changing room.

As I waited for her to change, I paced outside the door, thinking of my dad's face if he knew this was happening.

Two minutes later, my mother emerged, looking *stunning*, positively radiant, like Cinderella about to go off to the ball. I wanted to cover up the full-length mirror with my hands so she wouldn't see how good she looked.

Her new friends raved. "You *have* to get that," Zhou Tai Tai gushed.

As she twirled around in the gorgeous red dress, I held my hands up for old times' sake.

"Eggplant!" I said, and pretend clicked, like I was holding a camera. It was this thing my mom and I liked to do, especially whenever we tried on something nice at the mall. We'd pretend to take a picture of it and say *eggplant* because that's what we used to say in China instead of *cheese*. It was just a fun game, because of course we couldn't actually buy the dress.

Except today my mother didn't smile. She pretended to not hear my "eggplant." Mrs. Zhou asked me what I was doing, and I quickly put down my hands.

"Nothing," I muttered, glancing at my mom. Why wasn't she into it?

My mom ducked back into the changing room. When she came out, she was wearing her normal clothes and holding the red dress on the hanger. As she was about to put it back on the rack, Mrs. Zhou stopped her and said, "You're *not* going to get that?"

The other women all chimed in.

"It would be *criminal* not to get that dress!"

"Red's such a good color on you!"

"If I had your figure, I would buy two!"

My head bounced from tai tai to tai tai, not sure which of their statements I should refute first. Before I knew it, we were at the checkout counter. I watched in horror as my mom pulled out the crumpled bills from her purse—$187.99, *plus tax*. There was no discussion. There was no pause. There was no asking me what I thought. She just slid the cash across the counter like it was Monopoly money.

As the saleslady happily wrapped up the dress, I felt tiny bumps of panic all up and down my arms. *Dad is not going to like this!*

Hank was waiting for us at the store entrance when we walked out, wearing a brand-new outfit: a crisp white button-down shirt, fitted tan blazer, and smart gray slacks. His new shiny leather shoes clicked on the marble floor as he made his way over to us.

"Whoa!" I said when I spotted him. "You look amazing!"

Hank chuckled. "Do I clean up real nice or what?"

My mother's new friends stared at Hank. "Is *he* your husband?" Mrs. Zhou asked my mom, alarmed.

"No," my mom quickly said.

Mrs. Zhou put a hand over her chest and exhaled, like *thank God*. Hank, who couldn't understand a word of Mandarin, smiled politely at the women. As Mrs. Zhou and the others exchanged numbers with my mom, I was still thinking about Mrs. Zhou's question—*Is he your husband?* Why'd she have to make that face?

In the car on the way home, I gave my mom the silent treatment. I was mad at her for not sticking to the clearance section and buying a dress on sale, for not posing for my camera when I said *eggplant*, and most of all, for making friends with those horrible snobs.

But my mom was unusually quiet too. As Hank drove, she looked out the window. I wondered if she was thinking about my dad and the fight that they were definitely going to have. I could

almost hear the thunder in the car and nibbled my cheek in anticipation of the downpour.

Back at the motel, my mother tried to smuggle the shopping bag
into the manager's quarters without my dad noticing, but of course
he spotted it.

"What'd you get?" he asked.

Hank and I glanced at each other. I pointed at Hank's new
leather shoes, trying to distract him. "Look, Dad! Aren't they
cool?" I asked.

"They feel good too," Hank added, stomping around on the
carpet.

But my dad wasn't interested in Hank's shoes. "Oh, c'mon,
let me see what you got," he pressed my mom. He walked over
and reached for the bag, and before she could stop him — she
tried to hold it out of reach, but he was too fast — he pulled out
the dress.

We all watched as my dad touched the satin, his coarse hands
moving like needles against the soft fabric. "You got this on
clearance?"

She pressed her lips together, a self-imposed silence.

My dad looked at her, puzzled, and asked, "When are you ever
going to wear this?"

"I'll wear it!" my mom insisted.

But before she could say any more, my dad spotted the price tag,
and it was like KA-*BOOM*!

"Two hundred dollars for a dress? Are you *crazy*?" he yelled. He
stuffed it into the bag. "You're taking this back."

My dad was furious, and so was I — mad and scared. Was this

what my mom was going to do with her new credit card? Swipe and sign all our money away?

"It's my money too!" Mom yelled back. "I work hard for it. And on top of that, I have to do the housework *and* cook all the meals."

"But you like cooking the meals," my dad said.

"I don't *like* cooking the meals!"

I thought about all the nights my mom stood over the hot stove after a long day of cleaning. Sometimes, she'd pull out pieces of paper with math formulas written on them from her pockets and look at them while she cooked. Or she'd sew up a hole in my backpack while keeping an eye on the rice. My anger at her thawed a little.

Hank stepped in. "It's okay. We'll make the money back tomorrow. I promise. I work here now, remember?" Hank rubbed his hands together. "I'm going to give this motel a little something I like to call the *Hank magic*."

As Hank bid us a good night and clicked back to his room in his new leather shoes, my mom sat down on the sofa and lovingly stroked her new dress. "Okay, maybe it was a bit much, buying it in one go. Next time, I'll put it on a payment plan on my credit card," she muttered.

My dad's jaw dropped. "You applied for a credit card? I thought we talked about it!"

"No, *you* talked about it. *You* decided," my mom said, crossing her arms.

My dad fumed as he walked over to the cash register. "You think all that money in there is ours?" he asked my mom. "It's not ours. It belongs to many, many investors, all of whom need to get paid before we do."

"Yeah, and you always think about everyone else before your own wife!" Mom cried, reaching for a tissue. Tears glistened in her eyes.

"You guys!" I exclaimed. I was sick of all the fighting, and besides, as soon as Dad mentioned our investors, I remembered we had much bigger problems right now. "I have something to tell you."

My parents both looked up.

"Lupe and her dad can't be on our insurance plan," I said.

My dad looked taken aback. "Why not?" he asked.

I shifted my weight from one foot to the other, remembering that Lupe had sworn me to secrecy. "They . . . uh . . . they already got another one."

My dad took a seat on the couch next to my mom.

"There's got to be another plan we can enroll in," my mom said. "One requiring fewer employees."

My dad shook his head. "The other plans all have high deductibles. We can't afford them." Softly, he said to my mom, his eyes downcast, "See, this is why we can't just start living large. Our situation really hasn't changed *that* much. We have to be responsible."

My mom held her soft satin dress tight in her hands and sighed.

"Maybe tomorrow I can go and return it," she said. Then she turned to my dad and asked hopefully, "Do you want to see me try it on?"

My dad looked hesitantly at the dress.

"She really looks great in it," I said.

"Okay," my dad sighed. "But just *try*."

CHAPTER 10

On Friday at school, Mrs. Welch passed back our essays on immigration from the first day. I was excited to see what I got. I had written about America being a nation of immigrants. Our founders were immigrants. They worked hard to create a country that would welcome everyone. It said so right on the Statue of Liberty.

Cautiously, I turned my paper over, hoping to find an A or at least a B+. But there staring back at me was a big fat C.

I blinked at the page. I didn't get it. I was right back to where I started last year.

I turned to Mrs. Welch, who was still handing back essays. She asked some of the students to repeat their names for her. As they did, a curious thing happened. Kareña said her name was Karina. Jorge called himself George. And Tomás said Thomas. Since when did they start saying their names so . . . white?

After all the papers were passed out, Mrs. Welch went back to her seat. I looked down at the C, wondering whether I should just let it go. There wasn't a note from Mrs. Welch about why I got what I got. I couldn't help but wonder if it had anything to do with what I said in class earlier in the week. I glanced over at Lupe, who was busy studying her own essay.

At recess, I waited until everyone else was out of the class before hesitantly walking up to Mrs. Welch.

"Um . . . Mrs. Welch . . . can I talk to you about my essay?" I asked.

She looked up at me from her desk and took off her reading glasses.

"What about it?" she asked.

"I just . . . I was wondering why I got a C?"

Mrs. Welch's face tightened, like the lady at the checkout counter whenever my mom questioned her about giving her the wrong change.

"It's just that I thought I was good at writing. Last year, I even won —"

"I know," Mrs. Welch interrupted. "Mrs. Douglas told me before she moved away. But this is sixth grade. And I have higher expectations for what I consider an A paper."

I swallowed. Mrs. Welch returned to her grading, and I dragged myself out of the classroom. As soon as I spotted Lupe sitting under a tree and drawing in her sketch pad, I ran over and told her what Mrs. Welch had said.

"It's going to be fine," she said. "You've been through this before. Last year, remember?"

"Yeah," I said. "But I was kind of hoping I'd start good this year, you know? And end up amazing."

"You will," Lupe promised, shading in the trees in her drawing.

I watched her as she sketched, wondering if I should say what had been on my mind ever since she'd told me her secret. "Why didn't you tell me sooner that you were undocumented?"

Lupe put down her drawing pad and lay down on the grass. She put her hand under her head, and I stretched out next to her. We gazed up at the red and gold leaves that formed a roof over us. The wind blew and the colorful roof moved.

"I didn't want you to think I was different," she admitted. "I didn't want you to stop looking up to me."

"Oh, Lupe," I said, flipping onto my stomach. "I still look up to you! I'll always look up to you."

Lupe smiled. I plucked a blade of grass with my fingers.

"What's it like . . . to be undocumented?" I asked.

Lupe was quiet a long time, playing with her drawing pencil in her fingers.

"It's like being a pencil, when everyone else is a pen," she finally said. "You worry you can be erased anytime."

• • •

I was still thinking about Lupe's words when Jason's mom came to pick us up after school. Lupe dashed out of the parking lot as soon as she saw Mrs. Yao's white Mercedes, desperate not to bump into her.

"How was school?" Mrs. Yao asked.

"It was okay," I lied, climbing into the car. Though I was still pretty bummed about my C, the last people I wanted to tell my problems to were the Yaos. Jason climbed in, shoving our backpacks into the front seat so we'd have more space. Still, he sat alarmingly close to me.

"Wait till you hear what I have planned for us," he said with a grin.

Jason's house was even bigger than I remembered. As he gave me a tour, I found myself wondering how many people could sleep in each room and how much we could charge if we rented it out. *Definitely* more than twenty dollars a night.

Jason's room had a pinball machine, a big-screen TV hooked up to a video-game console, and a fish tank that spanned one entire wall. There was even a reading nook by the window. A chair with a built-in bookshelf full of books, right under the seat, sat invitingly in the sun.

"This is the coolest thing I've ever seen!" I said, sitting down on the chair, which was surprisingly comfortable.

"I don't really use it," he said. "If you want it, you can have it!"

"What?" I shook my head.

"No, I'm serious. If you see anything you like, just take it." Then Jason started taking books out of his book chair and handing them to me. "Here, take 'em."

I pushed them back. "Jason, I'm not here to take your stuff."

Jason blushed. There was a moment of silence.

"Right," he said at last. "I'm just . . . I'm really glad you're here."

Then I spotted a *Wilson for Governor* postcard on his desk. Jason followed my gaze and quickly explained, "My dad put that there." He walked over and turned the postcard facedown. "I don't really care who wins," he added.

"You should care," I told him. "Wilson wants to kick kids out of school. Make it impossible for them to go to the hospital."

"Only illegal immigrants," Jason said with a shrug. "They don't belong here anyway. My dad says they're costing the California economy. He's losing a lot of money on some of his businesses, you know."

I couldn't care less about Mr. Yao's losses. Instead, my chest rose and fell at the way Jason was talking about my best friend. "What does 'belong here' even mean?" I shot back. "Do *we* belong here?"

Jason shrugged again. "Of course we belong here. We *flew* here." As if to demonstrate, he took a piece of paper, folded it into an airplane, and flew it at me.

"So?" I asked, ducking the plane.

"So that means we had to get visas and stuff. We didn't just walk over. How would you like it if I just walked into your house whenever I wanted?"

I crossed my arms.

"Well, you kind of did. All last year," I reminded him. "You and your dad just showed up whenever you wanted."

"That was different—" Jason started to say. But the rest of his sentence was drowned out by his mother's voice, calling us from the kitchen.

"Jason! Mia!" Mrs. Yao shouted.

Jason leaped up from his chair. "To be continued," he announced. "I have to go make dinner."

I followed Jason into the kitchen, curious about his culinary skills. Were they for real? I couldn't imagine Jason cooking anything more than a Bored Sandwich: two slices of *I'm tired* with a thick piece of *uninterested* in the middle.

But tired he was not. Once in the kitchen, Jason transformed before my very eyes into a whole other person, a culinary wonder! I watched as he bounced from pot to pan, smelling this herb and sprinkling that spice, his hands chopping, stirring, dicing, and peeling on the marble countertop.

"The key is to take the pasta out before it gets too soft and immediately run it under cold water so it stops cooking," he said, turning on the faucet as he got ready to lift the towering, boiling pot. It was twice the size of his head, yet he seemed determined to move it all by himself.

"Stand back!" he cautioned.

"No, let me!" his mom offered, running over.

By the time she came around the counter, Jason had already masterfully lifted and emptied the pot into the colander in the sink.

While the pasta cooled, he moved on to a thick tomato sauce simmering on the stove. It was made from scratch, except that it wasn't a traditional spaghetti sauce. Jason had jazzed it up with Asian spices like Sichuan numbing peppers, which he fried in olive oil, filling up the entire house with a wonderful spicy smell, before sprinkling the oil into the sauce. I had to admit, I was impressed. Jason might look like a mad scientist, but it was pretty cool what he was doing!

"How do you come up with these recipes?" I asked.

Jason explained as his mom went to set the table, "I just really like food." He patted his plump tummy. "I like messing around in the kitchen, experimenting with different ingredients, seeing what works, what doesn't work." He pointed to the salt shaker, and I handed it to him. "It's like you and your writing."

My face fell a little, thinking about my C. "Yeah, well, lately my writing hasn't been all that great," I muttered.

"What are you talking about? It's amazing!"

"Mrs. Welch isn't exactly a fan," I admitted sheepishly.

Jason put the salt shaker down and looked into my eyes. "You can't do it for other people, you know. You gotta do it for yourself," he said. I furrowed my eyebrows, not sure what he meant. As if to demonstrate, Jason scooped up a spoonful of his sauce, lifted it to his mouth, and tasted it. "Mmmmmm."

I giggled. Just then, the front door opened and my least favorite voice in the world came thundering in.

"I'm home!" Mr. Yao announced.

CHAPTER 11

"You won't believe the day I've had. Dinner ready yet?" Mr. Yao called out.

No! He's not supposed to be here! I looked around for a place to hide as Jason's dad came into the kitchen. For a second, I thought about throwing the spaghetti over my head and pretending to be a mop. Too late. Mr. Yao took one look at me and narrowed his eyes.

"What's *she* doing here?"

Mrs. Yao walked in and put a hand on her husband's shoulder. "You remember Mia." She took his briefcase and his jacket from him.

"Do I remember Mia?" Mr. Yao snorted.

"She's staying for dinner!" Jason told his dad. Mr. Yao's face hardened like garlic that's been left out for too long, and I looked down at my feet.

"You know what, I'm not really that hungry. . . ." I started to say.

"What?" Jason protested, putting down the spatula. "You're not leaving, are you?"

I felt bad. He'd gone through so much trouble to make all the food.

Mr. Yao reached for another plate. "No, she's not," he said, glancing at me. "Come on, let's eat."

. . .

The Yaos' dining room, like everything else about their house, was massive and over the top. The mahogany dining table had one of those lazy Susans like at Chinese restaurants, except unlike at Chinese restaurants, the Yaos' table had a white linen tablecloth and silver cutlery and jade chopsticks shined to perfection.

I looked up at the crystal chandelier hanging just overhead, my mouth opening slightly as I stared at the kaleidoscope of colors. Mr. Yao and Jason took a seat, and Jason's mom set down the food. I took a bite of Jason's Asian fusion spaghetti, not quite sure what to expect. The tangy numbing peppers exploded in my mouth. *Wow.* It was unlike anything I'd ever tasted before. I turned and gave Jason a thumbs-up.

His dad, on the other hand, wolfed down the delicate pasta like it was cereal.

"Isn't this delicious?" Mrs. Yao said. "Would anyone like seconds?"

It really was spectacular, way better than the free school spaghetti, the only other Italian-style pasta I'd ever had. "You could be a chef!" I said to Jason.

He grinned.

"Don't get any ideas." Mr. Yao stabbed at the sautéed vegetables with his fork, then pointed it at Jason. "You're going to be a lawyer or a doctor when you grow up."

"Awww . . . what's wrong with being a chef?" Jason asked.

"It's a step down," Mr. Yao explained as he chewed. "It's what your grandfather did when he first came to this country. You know how hard it was for him to claw his way out? Now you want to go *back* in the kitchen?"

I could feel Jason's confidence shrivel like the spinach on my plate. He stared down at his fork.

Mr. Yao turned to me. "So how's my motel?"

I cleared my throat, eager for the chance to brag. "*My* motel is good. We've been full a few nights this summer. No vacancy."

"No vacancy?" Mrs. Yao said, impressed. She poured more red wine into her husband's glass. "Well, that's a surprise. We never used to get those, did we?"

Mr. Yao wiped the sauce off his frown with his napkin, then threw it on the table. "That's because they were too busy plotting against me to do any real work," he complained, grabbing a piece of bread.

I felt the anger pooling in my chest. *No real work?* What did he call all those sleepless nights? The million and one pillowcases my parents changed? My throbbing finger that I nearly rubbed raw making new keys?

"Dad!" Jason blurted.

"And let me tell you something," Mr. Yao continued, ignoring his son. "The circus of people you have owning that place — a bunch of immigrants, half of whom can't even speak English, random people off the street, the weeklies, and that guy, what's his name? Hank? It's never going to work."

"Hank now works at the motel as the Director of Marketing," I said matter-of-factly.

"*Director of Marketing?*" Mr. Yao exclaimed, spitting out his wine. He threw his hands up. "You know what, I can't listen to this."

I glared at Mr. Yao, feeling my composure unknot. "You're just mad that we won."

He burst out laughing. "You think that just because you had a couple of good nights this summer, you *won*?" Tiny bits of tomato sauce flew from his mouth and landed on my nose.

"Dad!" Jason said again, looking panicked.

"You know nothing about running a business!" Mr. Yao said. "You're a mere servant masquerading as a boss!"

The room went silent. I sat with Mr. Yao's words, feeling the tangy tomatoes sour in my stomach. It got so quiet, I could hear the dinging of the crystals on the chandelier above as they lightly tapped one another.

Slowly, I put my napkin down and got up from the dinner table.

"Mia, where are you going?" Jason asked.

I ignored Jason and went to his room to get my jacket. I couldn't believe I thought that maybe this time Mr. Yao would be different. That he might view me as an equal, a professional, his industry peer—when clearly, I had never advanced past hired help in his eyes.

Jason caught up with me as I reached the front door and followed me out to the driveway, leaving the door open behind him.

"Look, I'm sorry about what my dad said. He hasn't been himself lately. You gotta understand, all his investments are down—"

"Good," I said bitterly. "I hope they all tank."

It was mean, but I didn't care.

Jason looked down at his feet. His mom and dad called him from the dining room but he just stood there, socked feet glued to the cement, looking so tragically sad that I almost wanted to turn around and go back inside. Maybe the sweetness of his dessert would erase the bitterness of his dad's words.

Then I remembered that I didn't have to put up with Mr. Yao's words anymore — that was the best part about owning the Calivista — and I kept walking.

CHAPTER 12

I sat on the back staircase fuming when I got home. Lupe was right, I should have never gone over to Mr. Yao's house. People don't change. I heard footsteps coming my way and looked up to see José.

"You okay?" he asked gently. When I didn't reply, José set down his tools and took a seat next to me.

"Is it Lupe?" he asked. "Something happen at school?"

I shook my head. "No, it's Mr. Yao," I said. José raised an eyebrow. I groaned and told him what happened at dinner.

José shook his head. "Lemme tell you a story," he said.

Unlike Hank, José was a man of few words. So when he had something to say, you knew it was important. I sat up straighter in the moonlight.

"Eight years ago," José began, "when we first came over from Mexico, my wife and I worked in the fields, picking grapes. It was very, very hard. I was always coughing, because, you know, the grapes, there were many, many bugs, and they had to spray that . . . that . . . what you call that?" He paused, trying to describe with his hands.

"Pesticide?" I guessed.

"Sí, pesticide," José said, shuddering at the memory. "It was very bad for people. I wanted to find a better job, but my wife, she wanted to stay. She was scared. Lupe was very young then. Only three or four. My wife carried her on her back when she worked."

I smiled at the thought of little Lupe. She had never told me the story of her parents working in the fields when they first came.

"I didn't want Lupe smelling the pesticide, so I convinced my wife to quit and go to the city. Everybody said, 'José, you crazy. You not gonna find a job. You dreamin'.' But you know what?" José asked with a grin. "I found a job."

"Fixing the cable?" I asked.

"No, that was later. First, I found a job as a pizza boy," he said.

I smiled, thinking that sounded like a marvelous job, kneading the dough, throwing it in the air. But José said it wasn't fun at all, it was dangerous.

"Dangerous?" I asked.

"The pizza delivery place had a twenty-minute guarantee," he explained. "We will get your pizza to your house in twenty minutes, still hot, or your money back."

My eyes widened. That wasn't a lot of time.

"The white guys, they took the addresses that were close by," he said. "But I got the ones far away, *super* far away, way on the other side of town. No one can do it in twenty minutes."

"So what'd you do?"

"I tried," he said. I pictured José speeding down the city streets in his shaky truck with a piping hot pizza next to him. "Only thing we can do as immigrants is try, right?" he asked.

I nodded. "Right," I said. "And what happened if you didn't make it?"

"Then free pizza for the customer, and I must pay," he said. "I paid for many, many pizzas because I was five minutes late. One time, it was raining and I was driving very fast, and I nearly crashed."

I put my hands to my mouth and gasped.

"So I decided to get a better job. But it was not easy. Again, everybody told me, 'José, you not goin' get better job. You no skills,'" José said. He looked down at his tools and took a deep breath. "So I learned skills. I learned to fix the cable."

"Was that hard?" I asked him.

José nodded. "Oh, yeah. My first customer, I screwed up. I had to buy the guy a brand-new TV and pay for a professional to come fix it."

José winced, like even now, years later, it hurt. I thought of all the refunds I had to give our customers last year. They still hurt too.

Then his face brightened. "But I didn't give up. I kept practicing till I got it. And now I can fix any cable. And nobody can deny it, not even Yao."

I giggled, wishing an essay was like the cable, undeniable if it was good and working.

"I've known Yao a long time. Don't let his words get you down. You just have to keep proving him wrong."

"Thanks," I said. As he gathered up his tools, I looked over at him curiously and asked him a question that had been on my mind even before Lupe told me her secret. "Hey, José, why did you and your family decide to come here in the first place?"

José put a hand to his beard and gazed up at the stars. "I came here to give a better life for my daughter. A better education. Opportunities. Freedom."

I smiled. They were the same exact reasons my parents came here.

That night, I went to bed thinking about José and all the things he was willing to do to achieve his dreams, including racing across town with a pizza, and all the things I was going to do to achieve mine. I was determined to prove Mrs. Welch and Mr. Yao wrong.

• • •

On Saturday, my dad and I drove up the 5 Freeway toward the San Gabriel Valley in search of the shaved ice place that my dad said would bring me straight back to China. I wasn't sure I wanted to go straight back to China. I hadn't thought about my cousin Shen in months, which made me a little sad but mostly puzzled. He was like a brother to me growing up. Why didn't I miss Shen as much? Maybe because now I had Lupe.

"Wait till you see it! They have everything in Monterey Park," Dad gushed as he drove, practically giddy. "It's full of Chinese restaurants and grocery stores — even bigger than 99 Ranch!"

My dad loved the big Chinese grocery store near the motel. It kind of smelled like roasted char siu and spring onions, but I liked it. My parents insisted 99 Ranch was cheaper than the American grocery stores, but I think they just liked chatting with the butcher in Chinese.

"Tell me more about this shaved ice," I said. "What flavor are we going to get?"

"Red bean, of course."

Red *bean*? I wasn't sure I wanted any beans in my dessert.

"Don't you remember?" he asked. "I used to get it for you when you were a kid, and you'd eat it sitting up on my shoulders?" I shook my head, and he chuckled. "Well *I* remember. The ice would drip on my head! Your mother thought it was so funny."

I laughed, even though I didn't entirely remember. "Speaking of Mom, did she return her dress?" I asked.

"Oh, yeah, thank God they let her return it." He grinned. "Gotta love America!"

It took us forty minutes to get to Monterey Park, and when we did, my eyes boggled at the sight. There were *so many* Chinese people, all up and down the streets. I'd never seen that many people who looked like me, not even in Mrs. T's Wednesday classes. And what's more, all the restaurants were Chinese and even the signs were in Chinese!

"What *is* this place?" I asked my dad.

"You'll see." He smiled, getting out of the car. I scrambled after him, not wanting to get lost in this China outside China.

We went inside a shaved ice place called Lucky Desserts. It had one of those small cat figurines with the waving paw right by the entrance and a large poster of Buddha behind the cash register. I felt like I was stepping into my grandmother's kitchen or . . . my imagined version of my grandmother's kitchen. We left China almost four years ago, I realized. My memories were starting to get as cloudy as the shower doors in the Calivista guest rooms.

"We'll have two red bean ones!" Dad told the server in Chinese. As the server went to prepare the ices, my dad beamed at me. "You're gonna love this."

He drummed his fingers excitedly on the counter. I hadn't seen him this excited since the time we found a 1972 double-die penny worth $150!

The server presented us with two giant mountains of snow. Wild swirls of red and purple mounds, shaped like little Tic Tacs, rested on top. Excited to dig in, I grabbed a spoon, closed my eyes, and went for it.

The red bean tasted . . . like mashed potato. Mashed potato in ice. The tiny mounds sat on my tongue like little ladybugs. I made a face as I pushed them around in my mouth.

"What's the matter? You don't like it?" my dad asked, shoveling spoonfuls into his own mouth.

I willed myself to take another bite, for his sake, but it went down even worse, and almost came back up. Hesitantly, I shook my head.

"I'm sorry," I said, putting the shaved ice back on the counter. Gently, I told my dad, "I . . . I eat ice cream now."

I gazed up at his face, and the look that stared back made me want to grab the ice and jam it down my throat. But it was too late. He had already seen my true feelings.

"You eat ice cream now," my dad repeated.

"And chocolate chip cookies," I added in a small voice.

He nodded and put his own spoon down, as if suddenly, he didn't feel like eating anymore. As we stared at our two melting ices sitting on the counter, my dad shook his head and said with a sigh, "You and your mom are becoming so Americanized."

"No . . ." I started to say, and then stopped. What was wrong with becoming Americanized? "Isn't that what you wanted?" I asked my dad, looking into his eyes. "I mean, isn't that why you brought me here?"

My dad gave me a bittersweet smile. "I guess so. . . . I just hoped . . ." He sighed again. "I just hoped it would take a little while longer."

With that, he took the shaved ices and put them in the trash. It was the first time I'd ever seen him throw away food.

CHAPTER 13

On Sunday, I woke up to a crinkly noise beside me. I fluttered my eyelashes open to find a brown-and-silver bag next to my pillow and a note from my dad.

> Got you these. Maybe you can bake some cookies with Hank.
>
> Love,
> Dad

I grinned. They were semisweet chocolate chips for baking — and not the generic kind, the Hershey's ones! My dad must have gone out and gotten them after we got back from Monterey Park. I was so glad he wasn't still mad at me for not liking the red bean shaved ice and even more excited to make cookies for the very first time! I hugged the chocolate chips to my chest.

I'd never baked chocolate chip cookies before, but watching Jason had inspired my own culinary senses. I jumped out of bed and headed to the kitchen. I knew we had an oven, but we barely ever used it. Chinese cooking is usually just done on the stovetop. I opened up the dusty oven door and, sure enough, my mom was using it as an extra cabinet. There were cans of water chestnuts, baby corn, a bottle of soy sauce, and two extra TV remotes from the guest rooms all stashed in there. If anyone had turned the oven on, we would have had melted remote with a side of corn.

I was cleaning everything out when Hank walked into the kitchen. It was Sunday, his day off, and I knew he'd been planning to watch the Star Wars trilogy in his room, but maybe he'd be interested in some cookies to go along with that.

"Hey, Hank! Wanna help me make some cookies?" I held up the bag of chocolate chips.

"Sure!" Hank smiled. He started opening up all the cabinets looking for baking soda, brown sugar, and vanilla—none of which my mom had. We decided to go to the grocery store.

When I followed Hank out to his car in the parking lot, I noticed a sticker on the bumper: *Marketing Director of the Calivista Motel.*

"Nice!" I said to Hank, smiling and pointing at the sticker.

"Isn't it great?" Hank asked. "That way I can advertise the motel wherever I go!"

I grinned. Hank really was a marketing genius.

As he drove, we chatted about the customers that had checked in that week. Then he asked me how it went over at Mr. Yao's on Friday, and I made a face.

"That bad, huh?" he asked as we pulled into the grocery store parking lot.

I gave Hank the play-by-play as he pushed a shopping cart.

"I'm sorry," Hank said when I'd finished. "He always was a miserable grouch, that guy." He looked around the store. "All right, what do we need to get here?"

I read the ingredients from the recipe one by one as Hank loaded up the cart. When we were done, we walked back out to the parking lot. That's when I noticed it. The word *IMMIGRANTS* was spray-painted along the side of the grocery store, with a thick line through it. Underneath, someone had scribbled the words *Go back to your country*.

Hank dropped the plastic bag of groceries on the ground and immediately reached over to cover my eyes with his hand. But it was too late; I'd already seen. We walked toward Hank's car with our groceries trying to remain as calm as we could. The whole time, my heart hammered in my chest. I thought of the words *Go back to your country*. This *was* my country!

The sign, however, broadcasted loud and clear that a lot of people didn't feel that way.

· · ·

We were too shaken up to go straight home, so we headed to the park — the one we'd discovered over the summer, which sat on a hill right above Disneyland. If you looked closely, you could see the tip of Space Mountain, which Lupe and I still hadn't been to. We'd been hoping to go over the summer, but things were always too busy back at the motel.

Hank led me to a spot in the shade. "You okay?" he asked as we sat down underneath a tall oak tree.

"It's so mean." I shook my head, kicking the grass with my flip-flops.

"Things are at a fever pitch right now with the election."

I looked over at him. "But it's going to be okay, right?" I asked. "They're not *really* going to pass that law?"

"I hope not," Hank said, gazing into the horizon. A gentle breeze swept by us.

I fell quiet. He still didn't know about Lupe.

"What's the matter?" Hank asked. "Is it school?"

I groaned and started telling him about Mrs. Welch and my bad grade. When Hank heard what Mrs. Welch said about race not being real, he snorted.

"Race might be a social construct, but racism's as real as the clouds," he said, pointing at the sky. "You can see it, and you can feel it when it pours."

I thought about how true that was. We could see it plain as day. It was right there on the grocery store wall.

"Want to hear how my first week as Marketing Director went?" Hank asked. I nodded. "Well, I went to the bank. I wanted to try to get a line of credit for the motel, so if we ever need money, we can borrow it from the bank instead of turning to loan sharks."

"And?" I asked.

"And they turned me down." Hank sighed.

"Why?" I asked.

The leaves above rattled in the wind. Hank shook his head. "They didn't think they could trust someone like me to pay it back. I thought that if I got some nice clothes and dressed real smart, they'd treat me like everyone else . . . but it's not easy being a black professional."

Hank frowned into his hands. It hurt me so much to see him like this, and I wanted to run over to the bank and speak to the manager. Let 'em have a piece of my mind. And then take all their deposit slips and draw on them. Why did everything have to be so hard, even for Hank, who was born here?

Tears fell down my cheeks. Hank lifted his brown hand to rub them away. "Hey, it's okay," he said with a smile. "There are other banks."

I nodded.

"The point is, there are racist people everywhere. You can't avoid them, and you certainly can't let them stop you," he said. "You just have to hope that through your small interactions with them, eventually you'll change their minds."

I looked out at the clouds hovering above the Happiest Place on Earth. They were so thick and heavy in the sky, we could see them *and* feel them, even if we couldn't reach out and touch them.

Hank got up and reached out a hand. "Now how about we go home and make some chocolate chip cookies?"

I smiled.

CHAPTER 14

The cookies turned out great. I brought some to school to share the next day, but Lupe wasn't there. During art class, I snuck little bites when Mrs. Welch wasn't looking. We were talking about stylized art. One of the other kids raised a hand.

"Speaking of graffiti, is there a punishment for spraying stuff on a wall?" Jorge asked.

I put my cookie down and turned to him. *Did he see it too?*

"Are you talking about the graffiti outside Ralphs?" Tomás, or Thomas, asked.

"Wasn't it awful?" I asked.

"My mom says there was another one last month outside the Misión del Sagrado Corazón," Kareña chimed in, looking sadly down at her desk as she uttered the name of the local church.

My eyes bulged. "What did it say?" I asked.

"You don't want to know," Jorge said, shaking his head.

Mrs. Welch cleared her throat. "We're getting off topic," she said. "We're not talking about graffiti today; we're doing self-portraits. Now I need you to all get out a blank piece of paper and a pencil."

As we all dug out our pencil cases, I scribbled a note to Tomás, Kareña, and Jorge.

Meet me by the tree at recess.

−Mia

Mrs. Welch might not feel like talking about it, but I did.

· · ·

Under the green canopy of the tall oak tree, Kareña, Tomás, Jorge, and I sat exchanging info about the hateful words that'd been popping up all around town — not just on walls, but from people's mouths too — ever since Governor Wilson started airing his ads.

"My mom and I were in the laundromat, trying to do the wash," Kareña said. "This guy came in, told us to leave, and when we didn't, he opened up our machine and all the water came pouring out at us."

Tomás's hands clenched up tight.

"We had to grab our soaking wet clothes and run out!" Her chin quivered at the memory. "I nearly fell on the water."

"I'd like to wring that guy in the dryer," I fumed. "Was there anybody else there?"

"Yeah. There was a white family. But they just pulled their kids behind them and pretended not to see," Kareña said.

"That's the worst." Jorge shook his head. "The people who just watch and don't do anything."

I thought about all the times last year when Jason made fun of my clothes and nobody stepped in, not even Lupe. At the time I was really hurt that Lupe didn't stand up for me. Now I understood a little more why she might have been scared.

"Are you guys worried about Prop 187?" I asked them gingerly.

They jerked backward a little at the question. "We're not illegals, you know," Kareña said.

I waved my hands—that hadn't been what I meant. "I'm just saying, it affects, you know, all of us."

Kareña nodded. "Yeah, it does. Even if my family is safe, my aunts and uncles might not be." She sat cross-legged on the grass, with her chin in her hands. "I just think it's wrong, you know? That my little cousins won't be able to go to school."

"Or my auntie Ling's cousin's kid," I added.

Jorge nodded. "It's *so* wrong. And who's next? What if one day all immigrants aren't allowed to go to school?"

The recess bell rang. We peered back toward the classroom, sorry that our time under the peaceful tree had to end.

"This was nice," Tomás said.

"We should do this again tomorrow," Jorge suggested.

"Totally!" I smiled. "And my friend Lupe will be back tomorrow. She'll love our new secret club!" I liked the sound of that, a secret club.

"What do we call it?" Kareña asked.

I put a finger to my chin and thought real hard, even though Mrs. Welch was blowing the whistle at us to come back.

"How about Kids for Kids?" I suggested.

The others liked the sound of that. We shook hands on it and agreed to meet again tomorrow, under the leafy tree.

• • •

When I got home, a reporter from the *Anaheim Times* was waiting in the front office. Annie Collins explained that she had overheard Hank talking to the ad department when he came in the other day, and while she couldn't sell him an ad, she'd love to do a piece on immigrants and weekly residents banding together to buy a motel.

At the sound of the words *feature story*, Hank's eyebrows shot up. He immediately jumped into action, showing the reporter around the motel and introducing her to the customers, my parents, and the other weeklies, while I speed-dialed Lupe. Where was she? She did *not* want to miss this.

"Hey, it's me! Why weren't you at school today? Anyway, you won't believe it, but a reporter from the paper is here and she's interviewing all of us for a story," I said breathlessly. "Come quick!"

Lupe shrieked in equal excitement on the other end and put the phone down to go ask her parents. When she came back on, she said in a sad voice, "I'm sorry, I can't. My parents don't think it's a good idea for us to be in the paper . . . given the circumstances."

She sounded truly bummed.

"*No*, it's okay. . . ." I tried to persuade her. "She's not going to ask about that!"

"I'm sorry," Lupe said. "Plus, my grandma's sick. It's just not a good time right now. I have to go."

I sighed as she hung up the phone.

There was a knock on the glass door. "You ready, Mia?" Annie asked.

It was my turn to be interviewed. My palms started sweating; I hadn't thought at all about what I was going to say!

I followed Annie out to the pool area, where my parents and the weeklies were gathered. My mom was in her best pale blue linen dress, not as nice as the bright red satin one she had to return, but still lovely. She was sitting next to my dad, who had dug something out of his suitcase of clothes from China. He smelled of mothballs and mouthwash. Annie turned to me with her reporter notebook and pen.

"So, Mia, how old are you?" she asked.

"I'm eleven."

"What's it like working at the front desk of a motel as an eleven-year-old?"

I told Annie about my day-to-day duties and some of the difficulties I had at first, like trying to get the adults to take me seriously.

"But I'm better at that now," I said, glancing at my parents, who looked on proudly.

"I bet you are," Annie said as she scribbled. I noticed she was writing in shorthand, scribbles that only she could read. Like her own secret language. My eyes widened, fascinated. I'd never seen a real writer in action before!

"What do you like the most about working at the Calivista?" Annie asked me. Her eyes twinkled. "What do you think makes it special?"

I closed my eyes for a second, thinking about the question. There are so many things that make the Calivista special to me, but if I had to pick one . . .

"Here we treat everyone like family," I said. "No matter who you are and where you came from. That's what makes it special to me."

Annie smiled. "That's a beautiful answer!" she exclaimed. "And do you think we need more of that right now in California?"

I nodded. "Oh, yes." I thought about the lines from my essay on immigration, wanting to say them but hesitating because I didn't want to get another C in real life. But then I remembered what Jason said when I went over to his house, how it didn't matter what grade I got, if *I* liked something, that should be enough. So I cleared my throat and added, "America is a nation of immigrants. Our founders were immigrants. They worked hard to create a country that would welcome everyone. It says so on the Statue of Liberty."

Annie's bright eyes sparkled in surprise. "Well said."

I looked over at my dad, who wiped his eyes with the sleeve of his old checkered shirt.

Annie closed her notebook and announced she was all finished. As she was leaving, I asked her how she became a writer.

"I wrote a lot as a kid and eventually got published," she said.

"Published?" That seemed like the moon to me. "Like a book?"

"Like writing letters to the editor and submitting them to newspapers."

When she said that, I almost jumped into the air.

"I *love* letters!" I squealed.

I felt my heart fill with possibility. It was the most validating day ever! Listening to Annie talk about being a professional writer, fireworks exploded inside me even louder than the fireworks at Disneyland! The only thing that could have made the day better was if Lupe had been there.

CHAPTER 15

The next day at school, I told Lupe all about Annie, the reporter. I could tell she was super disappointed to have missed out on the opportunity, so I hoped the excitement of our new club would cheer her up. At recess, when I led her over to the tree, there weren't three kids there. There were six! Kareña, Tomás, and Jorge had each told a friend. Our club was growing!

Lupe grinned and got out her sketchbook to draw our new club logo while I welcomed the new members, Rajiv, Hector, and Sophia, under the tree. Once we were all introduced, we decided on the club rules:

1. Be gentle, be kind.
2. Say what's on your mind.
3. Cone of silence!!

As far as number two went, I wasn't sure how much Lupe wanted to tell the group. When it was her turn to share, she talked about how her grandmother was sick in Mexico, but she couldn't visit her.

"Why can't you visit her?" Sophia asked.

Lupe gazed at the leaves that had fallen onto the ground.

I immediately jumped in. "Uh, because their car's in the shop, right, Lupe?"

Lupe quickly nodded. "Yeah, and also my parents work all the time," she said.

About halfway through recess, Jason strolled over to our group. "Can I join?" he asked.

I looked to the others, who politely scooted over. Lupe scooted the slowest, moving like a sloth. I knew she wasn't crazy about him being there, but there were no hard and fast rules about who could join Kids for Kids. It was a club for everyone. That was the whole point.

"What are you guys doing?" Jason asked. "Having some sort of meeting?"

I nodded. "Yup, this is our new club."

Jason looked amused. "And what do you do in this new club?" he asked.

"We talk about what bothers us," Tomás told him.

Jason's eyebrows jumped. "That's *it*?"

We nodded.

"Seriously?"

Lupe crossed her arms. "If you're going to mock it—"

Jason held up his hands. "No, I'm not, I promise," he said.

We looked at him, and I could tell we were all trying to decide if he meant it.

As if to prove that he did, Jason said, "All right. You want to know what bothers me?" We nodded. "Mia here walked out on dinner at my house the other day."

"That was *so* not my fault!" I protested.

"It still hurt!" he shot back.

Lupe jumped in. "She didn't feel like staying. Why's it so important to you anyway?"

Everything got quiet, and I cringed. *Please, don't say you like me again!* I peeked at Jason.

Sweat beads lined up on his forehead. Finally, he blurted, "Because I'm having a hard time at school, okay? I kinda needed, you know, a friend."

My head jolted up in surprise. He never mentioned anything about having a hard time at school.

"Everyone in my class makes fun of me." He wrapped his arms around his middle to try to hide his body. "They call me a Chinese dough boy," Jason muttered. "Or a dumbling. Get it? Like dumpling but dumb."

When Jason said that, I felt my skin boil, as if they'd said that to me. Anger shot through my body — painful, stiff anger that I could feel all the way to my hot fingertips. I instantly felt bad for walking out on him at dinner.

We took turns telling Jason how sorry we were and how he shouldn't listen to those kids for even a second. When the recess bell rang, I lingered at the tree until everyone else left, so I could talk to him alone.

"Hey," I said. "I'm sorry I left your dinner the other day." Jason nodded, but didn't say anything, so I went on, "Maybe we can do it another time? Do you want to come over to the motel?"

He gazed up at the sun spots peeking through the leaves. "I don't know."

"You don't have to check anyone in," I promised. "Maybe you can show me how to cook!"

Jason's face brightened. "I'd like that! But shouldn't we do that at my house?"

I smiled, slightly amused. "We have pots and pans at the motel too, you know."

. . .

I thought about our new club on the way home. I'd had no idea that Jason was suffering so much in school. Why didn't he tell me about it that day when I came over? It was amazing what people kept all locked up inside . . . and what they let out under a breezy tree.

When I got back to the motel, I found a piece of mail waiting for me at the front desk.

It was a letter from my cousin Shen!

CHAPTER 16

Dear Mia,

How are you? I haven't heard from you for a long time. I hope you are well. My mom told me you guys bought a motel—that's so cool! We bought an apartment. We're now living in the second ring, closer to the town center. Do you still remember all the Beijing rings?

I bet when you come back, you won't even recognize Beijing. We have buildings now that shoot straight up to the sky! And malls with movie theaters and ice rinks in them! I'll have to take you to some when you come back. You WILL come back to visit, won't you? I miss you. Some of the other kids at my new school aren't so nice. They make fun of me for being from the fourth ring.

I'm sure when they meet my cousin from America, they'll shut up about their rings! Ha!

Yours,
Shen

I stared at the letter from Shen, feeling a little guilty for not writing to him in such a long time. I had no idea he missed me so much. I reread the letter, smiling a little at the memory of Beijing's geography.

There were eight rings in total, dividing the city in circular loops like the trunk of a tree. They went outward from the first ring, in the city center, where the emperor once lived, all the way out to the eighth, where folks who couldn't afford the city center lived. Beijing inner-ringers were notoriously snobby toward those from the outer rings, which seemed suddenly absurd from halfway across the world. I shook my head. Even when people are all from the same city, we find ways to divide ourselves. I wondered, if two people were from the same road, would they find ways to put each other down? "Well, *you're* from the left side of the street."

The telephone rang, jolting me from my thoughts. I answered it with my best customer service voice. "Calivista Motel, how may I direct your call?"

"Mia, it's me!" Lupe said. I could hear her sniffling. "My grand-mother passed away."

"Oh, Lupe, I'm so sorry!"

"My mom's going back to bury her," she cried. "And I'm just worried . . ."

I knew what she meant—that she didn't know how her mom was going to get back home after the visit. "Don't worry," I said. "We'll figure it out. Maybe we can persuade her not to go. . . ."

"It's too late," Lupe said. "She already left for San Diego."

. . .

After I got off the phone with Lupe, I sat at the desk, wishing there was something I could do. Something that would make Lupe feel better. My fingers fiddled with Shen's letter as I brainstormed, folding it and refolding it. I closed my eyes and tried to think back to my own great-grandmother's funeral in Beijing.

I ran out the back to go find my dad. I found him in room 7, setting up for his Lucky Penny search. As he laid the coins down, one by one and faceup, I told him about Lupe's grandmother.

"That's terrible," he said, the pennies momentarily forgotten.

"Do you still remember Tai Nai Nai's funeral?" I asked Dad gently. Tai nai nai was the Chinese term for great-grandmother on your dad's side.

My dad sat on the bed. "Yes, of course."

"What did we do at her funeral?" I asked. "Did we burn something?" My memory of Chinese rituals was fading, like the imprint of a customer's hand on the bathroom mirror. Still, I distinctly remembered the smell of burnt paper.

"Yes!" my dad declared, his face beaming. He looked so surprised. "You remembered!"

My dad told me that according to Chinese custom, people burn fake money at funerals, believing that the burning smoke will accompany the deceased into heaven. At Tai Nai Nai's funeral, we burned lots of fake money, making sure she had more than enough to live like a queen in the afterlife.

I knew what I wanted to do for Lupe's grandmother. That night, as my dad and the weeklies searched for the elusive 1943 copper alloy penny, I sat next to them drawing lots and lots of fake 1943 copper alloy pennies on pieces of paper. Each and every one of them was worth $40,000. I couldn't wait to give them to Lupe tomorrow. I just hoped there was a place in heaven where Lupe's grandmother could cash them.

CHAPTER 17

Lupe was so surprised the next day when I gave her all the fake stuff I drew for her grandmother, plus one hundred real dollars from my dad and a plateful of steamed sponge cake from my mom.

"What's all this?" she asked, looking down at my drawings of fake pennies, fake credit cards, a fake dog, a fake computer, a fake house, even a fake health insurance card—I *might* have gone a little overboard. But I wanted to make sure Lupe's grandmother was all set.

When I explained to her what the drawings were for, Lupe's voice hitched. "You drew all this for my abuelita?"

I nodded.

She held the drawings up to her chest. "Thank you. This means so much to me." Lupe leaned over for a hug as Mrs. Welch walked into the classroom.

"Look, students! Mia is in the paper!" she exclaimed, holding up that day's local newspaper. The headline read "Immigrants and Citizens Band Together to Buy Local Motel: The Calivista Under New Ownership."

"Let's see!" my classmates shouted, clamoring to get a closer look.

Lupe and I stretched our own necks out—we hadn't seen it yet either! There on the front page of the Metro section was a group picture of us out by the pool. I grinned at Lupe, whose face beamed with pride too.

"So you're a maid," Bethany said.

The room went silent. I could feel prickly heat spreading from my head all the way down to my legs.

"Uhhh . . . I manage the front desk of a motel," I said to the class. Blank faces stared back at me.

"So your *parents* are maids," Bethany clarified for the class. I glared at her. Ever since last year, when she was in my group for math and I lost us the challenge, she's had it out for me. "Well, aren't they?"

I turned away from Bethany, embarrassed and angry at myself for being embarrassed when I should have been proud. I looked over at Lupe, but since she wasn't in the photo or in the article, she was off the hook.

"I did not know this about you!" Mrs. Welch said, peering at me as though she had just discovered a shiny mint chocolate among her collection of stale candy corns. "Why didn't you tell us earlier?"

For precisely this reason!

"It says here you bought the motel with a bunch of immigrants," Scotty said. "What *kind* of immigrants?"

That did it. I exploded to the class, "The kind that works harder than all of you!" Turning to Bethany, I added, "All you do is sit there and braid your hair!"

Bethany dropped her jaw at me and pretended to look all hurt.

"Mia!" Mrs. Welch called. "That's quite enough! You're staying after school, and you're going to help me clean up the classroom!"

I slid in my chair, groaning. I couldn't believe it. Bethany practically called me a vacuum cleaner, but *I* was the one in trouble?

. . .

As soon as the classroom emptied that afternoon, Mrs. Welch put me to work: tidying up the bookshelf, wiping down the desks, reorganizing all our color pencils and markers, and picking up all the little pieces of paper off the floor.

There sure were a lot of little pieces of paper on the floor, like it hadn't been vacuumed in weeks. I wondered what happened to the school janitor.

"As you know, due to budget cuts, we've had to make a few staff changes," Mrs. Welch explained, reading my mind. She picked off the old Blu Tack still stuck on the board, which had hardened and turned into small rocks.

I wondered if that was what happened to the school librarian. I'd gone into the library several times looking for Mrs. Matthews since school started. She'd been so nice to me last year, helping me with my research, and I missed her, especially now that I was in Mrs. Welch's class. But every time I went to the library, there was just a parent volunteer sitting at her desk.

As we cleaned, Mrs. Welch asked me about my job at the motel. I tried to give her as few details as possible, worried she might be trying to turn my parents in for child labor. You never knew with Mrs. Welch.

"You shouldn't give your classmates such a hard time. They're just curious," she said.

They were so *not* "just curious," I wanted to say, but instead I crawled under Mrs. Welch's desk. I picked up a bunch of receipts by the side of her trash can for coloring pencils, dry erase markers, and other supplies — Mrs. Welch sure bought *a lot* of stuff for us. As I was picking them up, I noticed a frame hanging on the wall. It was sort of hidden behind her chair, low to the ground, so I'd never seen it from my seat. I leaned in to get a closer look and read the words *University of South Carolina* and underneath, Mrs. Welch's name and the words *Doctor of Philosophy*.

Mrs. Welch was a *doctor*? I crawled back out, put the receipts on her desk and looked up at her.

"What's wrong?" she asked.

"Nothing," I said.

She looked down at the receipts. "Thanks for picking that up, but you can throw them away." She added with a sigh, "The administration's not going to reimburse me for all that stuff. But I had to buy them for you guys."

I raised an eyebrow, thinking that was nice of her. As I threw the receipts out, Mrs. Welch took a walk around the classroom and declared, "Well, this looks pretty good." It did look better. The books on the bookshelf were straightened and all the markers put away. The papers on her desk were in a neat pile — Lupe's A+ math test on the top. My mom was right. Lupe was *great* at math.

Mrs. Welch walked over and plopped down on her chair, satisfied. "Good work, Mia. I hope next time you'll think before saying something in anger to your classmates. You can go home now."

I walked over and grabbed my backpack. I peered back at Mrs. Welch as I walked out of the room. She was hunched over in her favorite position, grading essays at her desk, her eagle eyes moving intensely across the page as she jabbed the paper gleefully with her red pen.

She looked up at me and added, "We're doing another essay next week. Hopefully you'll do better."

I nodded, eyes lingering on the degree behind her chair. I tried to picture her as a doctor and wondered which was scarier — having her decide on my grades or my medicine.

CHAPTER 18

Mrs. T, Mrs. Q, and all the weeklies were celebrating when I got back. Hank kissed the newspaper in his hand, shrieking, "Did you see, Mia? This is marketing gold!"

I giggled as he twirled me around in the front office. There was already a framed copy of the article on the wall, and Hank and I stood proudly next to it, while my dad called up all his immigrant buddies and bragged about the article, saying how we'd done it! We'd really made it in this country! Their enthusiasm was so contagious, I forgot all about my own classmates' earlier reactions.

"We're in the paper! We're in the paper!!" we sang as we danced around the motel. Hank ordered pizza while my mom set up tables out by the pool. My dad patted Hank on the back.

"This was all you, Hank," he said, smiling at him. "If you hadn't gone in to talk to the paper about the ad, the reporter would have never known about us."

Hank laughed. "It's what I'm always saying to Mia," he said, ruffling my hair. "You gotta keep trying!"

My parents held up cups of cream soda.

"To Hank!" they cheered.

"To the Calivista!" Hank replied.

• • •

Twenty minutes later, I was finishing up a letter to Shen (I included a copy of the article!), when the pizza arrived. I jumped down from the desk and joined my parents out by the pool. As I ate my slice by the side of the pool, I thought about Lupe and what she was doing. I wished she was here, but she said she had to stay by the phone in her house in case her mom called. Her mom was probably somewhere in Sonora, Mexico, by now. I saved a slice of pizza for Lupe. Maybe tomorrow we could microwave it in Fred's microwave and it would still be good.

My mom joined me on the edge of the pool. "Hey, do you know what a doctor of philosophy is?" I asked her.

"Yeah, why?" she asked, rolling up her cleaning pants and dangling her own tired feet in the water.

I groaned and told her about cleaning in Mrs. Welch's room. "But don't worry, it was a 'dry mess,' not a 'wet mess,' like some of our customers leave."

My mom smiled. "So what's this about a doctor of philosophy?"

"My teacher has one."

My mom nearly dropped her pizza in the pool. "Your teacher has a PhD?"

"*Ph*-what?" I asked. My eyes moved to the pool water, which we had to keep at a certain pH level or else the health department would come knocking. That was the only pH I knew.

"A PhD is what they call a doctor of philosophy," my mom explained. "It's one of the hardest degrees you can get. It's for teaching college."

"Wow. What's she doing teaching sixth grade, then?"

My mom gazed down at the pool, at the soft ripples reflecting the setting sun. "I guess it's kind of like me cleaning motel rooms, even though I was once an engineer."

I thought about that as I watched the clouds in the sky shift. I guess that would explain why Mrs. Welch was so mad all the time. If it was, it was a pretty silly reason. We might only be in sixth grade, but her students weren't chopped liver. Some of us were running businesses.

. . .

At school the next day, we gathered again underneath the big oak tree. There were ten of us now. Jason smiled and congratulated me on the article.

"We all saw it, even my dad," he said.

"Really? What'd he say?" I asked.

Jason paused and said, "Nothing, but I could tell he was proud." I knew he was making the proud part up but still, it felt good to hear.

"I'll tell Hank you said that," I said. "Better yet, you can tell everyone yourself when you come over this Friday!"

Timidly, Hector raised his hand. "I actually live in a motel too."

We all flipped our heads to him, me and Lupe especially. All this time, I thought I was the only one, that I was *so* not normal — which was why I never told anybody where I lived, not a single soul except Lupe, until the newspaper told *everyone*.

"We've been living in the Days Inn over on Ball ever since my dad lost his job," Hector said.

Rachel, one of our first white club members, piped up, "You're lucky. We've just been living in our car. We lost our home a few months ago to the bank."

All heads turned to Rachel, and she shrank in the grass. I knew just the feeling, that itchy, scary sensation that you've said too much and now nobody will ever look at you the same again.

"We've lived in our car too," I confessed.

"Well, I *sorta* live in a car," Tyler, another one of our new members, said. "It's called a trailer home."

"Like our classroom!" Lupe said.

Tyler grinned. "Yeah, just like our classroom."

As we all oohed and asked him questions about what it was like, Tyler chuckled and promised he'd have us over and show us.

Walking back to class that day, I couldn't believe it. This whole time, I thought I was the only one who didn't live in a big two-story house with a white picket fence. I had *no idea* there were so many others. The knowledge that I wasn't all alone made me feel so warm and fuzzy inside, I decided it was a good thing the paper ran the story. It made all the maid jokes I got from Bethany Brett worth it.

CHAPTER 19

Hank was carrying a gigantic box into the front office when I got home from school. He threw his Anaheim Angels baseball cap onto the desk, and both my mom and I looked up.

"Guess what I bought with my new credit card?" he beamed. "Ladies, may I introduce the newest, most state-of-the-art, top-of-the-line phone system!"

We gasped as Hank proceeded to pull out the fanciest electronic device I'd ever seen. My mom reached out and ran her fingers over the smooth surface. "I used to make these."

"No kidding!" Hank said.

"You bought this with your new credit card?" Mom asked him. She looked around the desk for today's mail, but all we'd gotten were some supermarket flyers. "I wonder where mine is."

As I played with the bubble wrap, my mom helped Hank set up the phone. Her long, slender fingers worked expertly as she plugged in this cord and that wire. When at last everything was connected, she switched on the power. The machine beeped to life. Hank clapped.

"It works!" he shouted.

My mom smiled as Hank complimented her electronic assembling skills, even though I could tell she was also a little bit sad. It dawned on me then that maybe Mom missed more about her old life than just shopping — after all, she didn't used to just turn these on, she *made* them.

. . .

I found Mom sitting by the pool later that night, a letter in her hand. I saw it was from the Visa company and my eyes widened.

"Is it your new credit card?"

She shook her head. "Your dad didn't want me to find this. He didn't want me to be upset." She handed me the letter.

> Dear Ms. Ying Tang,
>
> Thank you for your interest in a Visa credit card. We're sorry to inform you that your application for a Visa credit card has been rejected. We cannot approve your application for the following reason:
>
> Not enough accounts opened long enough to establish a credit history.
>
> Please contact us again in the future when you feel your circumstances have changed. We look forward to reevaluating your credit card application at that time.
>
> Sincerely,
> Visa

"This is dog fart!" I exclaimed. "They're punishing you for not having enough of a credit history? How are you supposed to *get* a credit history if you can't get a credit card?"

My mom wiped her eyes with her sleeve, got up, and tossed the letter in the pool trash can.

She was quiet the rest of the night. To cheer her up, I offered to make math worksheets with her, and Dad tried making her his own "credit card," a piece of paper that was good for not having to cook dinner. All she'd have to do is flash the card, and he'd whip up something for us.

"Thanks," Mom said. "I appreciate that." But she looked down at her hands, cracking and peeling from cleaning rooms all day long, and sighed. "I just wanted to have a credit card, like everyone else. And be able to accumulate miles and maybe take our family on a free vacation."

"I know," Dad said, giving her a hug. I wrapped my arms around both of them and squeezed my parents tight.

. . .

That night, I fished the letter out of the trash. I intended to write the Visa people a letter of my own.

Dear Visa,

You say you're "everywhere you want to be." You know where you're not? In the hands of the hardest-working person I know. A first-generation immigrant. Someone who cleans thirty rooms a day and <u>still</u> has time to teach immigrant kids math every week.

That person is my mom, Ying Tang, a person you just rejected because she didn't open enough accounts to establish a credit history. Well, she's been busy. She's been busy taking care of a motel, which she <u>BOUGHT</u> after having worked there as an employee for a year. She's been busy raising me, helping her friends, looking after the weeklies, and cooking huge dinners for all of us, which now that I've baked chocolate chip cookies, I realize is actually a lot of work. That's what she's been doing, instead of opening up credit card accounts. So you can say all you want that she doesn't have a credit history, but that doesn't mean she has no credit. She has plenty of credit with the people around her.

I hope you'll reevaluate her application for a credit card. It'll mean a lot to her and to me.

Sincerely,
Mia Tang

Bright and early the next day, I mailed it.

CHAPTER 20

At school the next day, I found an envelope on my desk. It was a thank-you card from Lupe. Inside, she had drawn her grandmother sitting in the middle of a mansion, even bigger than Jason's house, with a pet Chihuahua and shiny lucky pennies at her feet. I smiled, looked over to Lupe, and put a hand over my heart.

The drawing was beautiful. Lupe had sketched her grandmother so vividly, every strand of her silvery hair shone as it flowed in long, curvy waves down her back.

"All right, class!" Mrs. Welch announced. "Clear your desks and get out your pencils. We're writing another essay. This one is about *what art means to you.*"

I immediately looked over at Lupe again. She sat so excitedly at her desk that her table wobbled. She was *so* pumped for this.

I turned to the blank piece of paper in front of me and took a deep breath. I was excited too — here was my second chance to prove my teacher wrong. I picked up my pencil and started writing.

But as I wrote, I kept getting distracted, thinking about my mom's credit card application and how hers got rejected but Hank's got approved, even though it was the first credit card application for both of them. I was *super* happy for Hank, of course. And he was so kind. As soon as he'd found out about my mom's rejection, he'd offered to let us use his card whenever we needed to.

"We could share!" he suggested. But we couldn't let him do that. A personal credit card was a personal credit card. Why did Hank get one and we didn't?

When I brought this up at my Kids for Kids club later, everyone had all sorts of ideas.

"Maybe they were talking about bank accounts. Maybe your mom didn't have a bank account for long enough?" Hector guessed.

I shrugged. "Beats me."

"These things are never fair," Juan said. "My grandma got rejected for Medicare, even though we're citizens and she totally qualified."

"My mom's still waiting for her green card application to get approved," Alicia sighed. "It's been taking so long."

I glanced over at Lupe. She still hadn't told any of the other kids her situation.

Hesitantly, she said, "My mom's in Mexico now to bury my grandmother. I'm worried they're not going to let her back in."

The other kids all let out a collective *been there* nod, and I smiled at Lupe, proud of her for letting out a piece, however small, of what had been weighing on her chest.

. . .

Later that day, several immigrants were gathered outside the front office, trying to get information on Mrs. T's How to Navigate America classes. One of the immigrants, Mr. Martinez, recognized the other guy, Mr. Rodriguez, who had brought his young son.

"Hey, it's you!" Uncle Martinez said to Uncle Rodriguez.

"Amigo!" Uncle Rodriguez greeted him.

Lupe and I looked at each other. "Have you guys already met?" I asked. They nodded and informed me they recognized each other from a job interview at a restaurant downtown. They'd both applied to be dishwashers.

"Did you get hired?" Uncle Martinez asked.

Uncle Rodriguez shook his head and looked down sadly. "No," he said. "Did you?"

Uncle Martinez sighed and shook his head too. "I spent an entire day washing dishes for the boss for free, hoping to get the job."

I thought about my dad's old job working at a restaurant and the blisters he brought home from frying rice in the wok all day long. I couldn't imagine doing that for free!

"Downtown? You guys talking about Felix over on La Palma?" Lupe asked.

They nodded.

"Sí, that's the place," Uncle Rodriguez said, pulling his young son close.

Lupe frowned. "My dad says never to go there. He's fixed their cable a few times. The boss never hires *anybody*."

"What do you mean, never hires anybody?" I asked.

"I mean every day, he interviews somebody for a dishwasher job and gets them to spend the whole day 'trying it out,'" Lupe explained. "But it's just a scam to get people to work for free. He's been doing it for years."

Uncle Rodriguez slapped his leg with his hand. "The tacaño!"

"And he's been doing this for *years*?" Uncle Rodriguez asked.

Lupe nodded. It was the worst thing I'd ever heard. Even worse than Mr. Yao, who at least hired somebody, though he squeezed us like lemons. I still remembered his words to my parents when they dared to complain: "If you don't want this job, there will be a thousand immigrants lined out the door to take your place!"

"You guys! We should turn this Felix guy in!" I looked around for a piece of paper and a pen. "I could write a letter right now —"

But Lupe, Uncle Rodriguez, and Uncle Martinez quickly shook their heads.

"No. No. No. Can't turn him in," they said. "Need papers to turn him in."

Oh.

Lupe locked eyes with me and explained, "That's why he can get away with it for so long. Because he knows these guys can't go to court; we don't have papers."

I realized something I'd never thought of before: that the thing I'd been relying on to voice my complaints and frustrations, my outlet and most powerful ammunition, wasn't available to everyone. There were certain things you needed to write letters, besides just a pen.

Uncle Rodriguez gazed at his son, who reached out and touched the Disneyland poster in our front office with his fingers. "We can only hope to make our kids' lives better," he said. Uncle Martinez nodded. "Through education . . . but now they're thinking of taking *that* away too."

"They won't," Lupe said. As she gave the uncles the information on Mrs. T and Mrs. Q's How to Navigate America class as well as my mom's math class, I knelt down and asked the little boy if he'd ever been to Disneyland.

"No . . ." he said. "But I want to go. It's right around here, right?" His bright eyes peered up at me with curiosity. "What's it like?"

I wished I could tell him it was just as nice as in the poster, but the truth was, I didn't know. "I haven't been yet either," I said to him. "But I hope I'll get to go soon."

"Me too," he said, slipping his small hand into mine.

CHAPTER 21

After Uncle Rodriguez and Uncle Martinez left and Lupe went home, Jason's mom dropped him off at the motel. We stood in the front office, waving as she backed out. She looked a little uneasy about leaving him, but I was excited. Jason was going to teach me how to cook!

We went straight to the kitchen, where Jason eyed my mother's spices, many of them hand carried from China, with fascination.

"Wow, look at all these!" he exclaimed. I grinned as he picked each and every bottle and jar up, opened them, and put them to his nose, like my mom did at the perfume counter at JCPenney. "So what do you want to make?" he asked. "How about something simple, like scrambled eggs?"

"I know how to make scrambled eggs," I said. "You just throw the egg in the pan, and then done."

Jason held up a finger. "Wrong. Not done," he said with a smile. He moved my mother's wok and reached for the flat skillet. It was fun watching him in his element, grabbing an egg from the fridge and cracking it into a bowl with one hand. I thought about what he'd said during the Kids for Kids club earlier in the week, about how the other kids in his class made fun of him. If only they could see him now.

As Jason stirred the egg, I lifted my hands and said, "Eggplant!"

Jason looked confused as I preterd clicked with my finger. "Eggplant?" he asked. "You want to put *eggplant* in your scrambled eggs?"

I chuckled and shook my head. "It's just something my mom and I say . . . or used to," I said, my face falling a little.

Jason grabbed a pair of chopsticks and started mixing up the egg. For a kid who was born and bred in America, he sure knew how to use chopsticks. My dad would be so impressed. When it came time to pour the egg mixture into the skillet, Jason reached for the cooking oil.

"No." I reached out to stop him, pointing instead to the small bowl just to the left of the stove. "Here, use this! It's leftover from last night."

"Ew!" said Jason, making a face. "How poor *are* you guys?"

I immediately looked away, kicking myself for inviting him here. He could be so *mean*. Just as I grabbed my dad's leftover oil and was about to pour it down the drain, Jason gently pried the bowl from my hand.

"Sorry," Jason said. He held the oil up to his nose and sniffed it. "Actually, it probably tastes pretty good, you know, because it's been infused with dinner and breakfast."

I looked up at him, surprised, as he poured the oil and the egg mixture into the pan.

"Now comes the magic!" Jason announced.

He reached for the spatula and started stirring like mad. He stirred every inch of the egg mixture continuously. In another minute Jason held up a taste for me on the spatula: creamy scrambled eggs that melted on my tongue.

"Mmmmmm," I said, closing my eyes. "You really should be a chef."

"Thanks!" He beamed. "I've been thinking of asking my parents if I can go to this cooking class in Irvine on the weekends. It's at the Orange County Kids Culinary Academy. I've been wanting to go there *forever*."

"You should totally do it!" I encouraged him. Jason's parents could definitely afford a fancy cooking school.

When we were done washing and putting all the dishes away, we went back over to the front office, where we sat in the late afternoon sun and flipped through yesterday's paper. I was reading the Letters to the Editor section while Jason scanned the Food section. A lot of the letters were about immigrants. People wrote in complaining that they took away their jobs. I wanted to say to these people: *How could they take away your jobs when they can't even get hired as dishwashers?*

I flipped the page and an article caught my eye.

"Hey, look at this!" I said to Jason, pointing. "There's a big march next month in downtown LA to protest Proposition 187. We should go!"

"No way." Jason frowned. "I'm not going to some crazy march." He gave me a serious look and added, "And neither should you. There'll probably be a bunch of racist people there, booing you. Is that what you want?"

"I don't care about them."

Jason shook his head at me, as if to say, *Well, you should.*

"This is serious, Jason. Kids might not be allowed to go to school if Prop 187 gets passed!"

"Yeah, but that's not going to happen to *us*."

I thought back to what my dad had said to his immigrant friends at Buffet Paradise. "We're all in the same boat."

"*I'm* not. Maybe you and Lupe are, but I was *born* here."

Sometimes, when Jason said stuff like that, I wanted to whack him upside the head with his own frying pan.

"You're still not white," I reminded him. Had he forgotten all the things he'd said in Kids for Kids about being the only Chinese boy in his class? Because *I* hadn't.

Jason fell quiet, his fingers wrinkling the newspaper. The Friday rush hour traffic hummed outside as cars sped down Coast Boulevard. Jason muttered, "I see your point."

I looked over at him as the phone system beeped. The screen showed it was my mom calling from room 14 — she needed me to bring her some stain remover and tape. I said sure, grabbed the Scotch tape, and ran out the back to the laundry room for the stain remover. Jason followed me.

We found my mom bent over room 14's bathroom sink, a bedsheet in her hands. A red wine stain — those were the worst.

"One of these days I'm going to rub my fingers raw," she muttered under her breath as she frantically scrubbed.

It was useless. The redness just kept spreading. She squirted the stain remover, but the dark wine clung stubbornly to the fabric threads, as if to stick out its maroon tongue and say, "Nah-nah nah-nah-nah."

"Give me the tape." Mom held out her hand.

But that didn't work either. Frustrated, she dropped the sheet on the floor and crouched beside it, like she was praying to the laundry gods.

Then out of nowhere, Jason suggested, "You could try milk!"

My mom gave him a funny look.

"I just remembered, I saw Lupe's mom do that once. When she used to clean for us," Jason explained. "She soaked a stain like that in milk."

Wait, what? Lupe's mom used to clean for the Yaos? Lupe never told me that!

My mom jumped up. "It's worth a shot. These sheets are brand new. We can't afford to throw them out. I'm going to the store right now — I'll be back in fifteen minutes!"

Halfway to the door, though, she paused. I remembered at the same moment: My dad was still at the Home Depot. We only had one car.

"A second car would be helpful at a time like this!" my mom muttered, shaking her head.

"Maybe Hank could take you," I suggested. "He's out by the pool, working on our bank loan applications."

"Good idea!" she said, and ran out.

Jason and I sat down on room 14's bed.

"I didn't know Lupe's mom used to clean for you guys," I said.

Jason shrugged. "It was a long time ago."

All sorts of questions sprouted in my mind. *When? For how long? Why did it stop? Why didn't either of you ever say anything about this before?* I didn't know which to ask first.

"She was a good cook," he went on. "Lupe and I used to watch her in the kitchen. My mom said her food was too spicy, but I liked it."

"Lupe would come with her mom?" My head was exploding. Lupe couldn't *stand* Jason. Why would she want to be at his house?

"Oh, yeah, all the time," Jason said. A nostalgic look crossed his face.

"Did . . . something happen?" I knew I was prying, but I couldn't help it.

He shrugged. Instead of answering me, he picked up a pillow from the bed. A mischievous smile appeared. "You know what I've always wanted to do in these rooms but my dad never let me?" Before I could answer, he hit me with the pillow.

"Hey!" I said. I wasn't going to let him get away with that. I picked up the other pillow and hit him back. Jason laughed.

We jumped on the bed and started having a pillow fight, laughing and screaming. Tiny little feathers leaked out of the pillows and fell around the room like snowflakes. They didn't seem like a big deal until it was too late—before I knew it, the feathers were *everywhere*.

"Oh, no!" I leaped off the bed and dropped to my knees, trying to pick up as many as I could. They were prickly little things, with tiny little sticks that poked my fingers.

Jason kept jumping, completely oblivious to the mess.

"You have to help me!" I shouted. "Get the vacuum cleaner!"

Finally, Jason hopped down. He was about to plug in the vacuum when I waved my hands and shouted, "WAIT!"

Our vacuum cleaner, much like our washing machine, was very old. I didn't know if it could handle a thousand spiky feathers poking it from the inside. And if it broke, would we have enough money to buy another one?

"Let's just pick them up with our hands," I said.

Jason made a face. "With our *hands*?"

I continued gathering them, one by one. Reluctantly, Jason joined me. He groaned and sighed as we picked. They were stubborn little critters. Whenever I put one in my palm, another one jumped off.

As we were kneeling and picking, the door opened. I looked up, expecting to see my mom back from the store, but instead I saw Mrs. Yao. She gasped at the sight of her son on the floor.

"What are you doing?" she yelped. "Get up!"

"We're just cleaning," I explained, but Mrs. Yao's porcelain skin had turned the same shade as the sheet stain. She looked like she wanted to grab Jason and strangle me.

"I didn't let him come over so he can be the maid!" she snapped. I felt my ears boil. Before I could say anything else, she turned to Jason. "Get in the car!"

As he walked out, Jason put the feathers he'd gathered in my hand. I stood very, very still, feeling the soft feathers in my palm, their ends like sharp, tiny knives.

CHAPTER 22

In the days leading up to October, a dark cloud settled over the state of California. Hank and I sat in the manager's quarters every evening, watching the news.

"Whether or not Prop 187 wins Wilson the election, one thing is clear," the newscaster said one night. "There has been an increase in hate crimes. In downtown Los Angeles, a Hispanic woman was shopping, and the store clerk refused to take her Visa card, saying it was probably a fake."

I shook my head, wanting to cover not just my ears but the ears of every other member of Kids for Kids. I hoped they weren't watching this.

"And in Northridge, a Latino man was asked to sit at the back of the bus," the newscaster went on. "This comes as a customer at a home improvement store was harassed by security guards in the parking lot, who threatened him with a baton."

I gasped, gooseflesh spidering up my arms as I thought about Lupe's mom and what might happen to her if she got caught trying to come back. She was still in Mexico, trying to find a coyote, which Lupe said wasn't a real coyote but a person who could lead her back through the desert and into the United States.

Hank switched off the TV. We sat in silence, listening to the hum of the refrigerator.

"I don't know about you, but I intend to volunteer at the ACLU on my day off," Hank said.

I nodded, thinking that was a good idea. I knew from reading the newspapers that the American Civil Liberties Union was a nonprofit organization that helped protect the rights and freedoms of people living in the US. I gazed out the window at the Calivista sign. "Hey, will you help me put something up on the sign?" I asked him.

"Sure."

Hank went out back to get the ladder as I chose the letters I wanted. As he climbed, I asked him to add two more words underneath *CALIVISTA MOTEL* and *AS SEEN ON TV*:

IMMIGRANTS WELCOME.

. . .

I thought about our new sign in class the next day. They were two little words, but seeing them lit up in the night had felt good.

Mrs. Welch passed back our essays. This time I got a B–. Still not great, but an improvement.

"What'd you get, Mia the maid?" Bethany Brett asked. Ugh. Ever since the article came out, she'd been calling me that.

"None of your business," I replied, quickly turning my paper over.

"Not like it matters. You don't need good grades for taking out the trash, right?" She laughed.

I was about to tell her off, when I thought, *Forget it*. I didn't want another cleaning session with Mrs. Fancy Degree.

My mom was in the manager's quarters putting away some keys when I got back.

"Was it your idea to put up that new message on the sign?" she asked, pointing out the window.

I nodded. "You like it?"

"I do," she said. I smiled.

I asked her if she had heard anything else from the credit card company. I'd been checking the mail every day since I sent them my letter. But her face fell and she said no.

To cheer her up, my dad suggested that she go out after the last room had been cleaned. "Take the night off," he said.

"You sure?" my mom asked.

She looked over at me, but my eyes were on the TV, where another Wilson ad was playing. Gunshots fired in the background and the scary voice announced, "Pete Wilson has the courage to say enough is enough!"

I clicked the TV off and jumped to my feet. "Can I come too?" I asked.

My mom nodded and walked over to the phone to call her friends that she'd made at the mall.

I groaned. "Why do we have to go with them?" I asked. "Can't we go with Auntie Ling or someone?"

"Auntie Ling's still working at the restaurant," my mom said as she dialed the number. "Besides, they're fine!"

Mrs. Zhou, Mrs. Li, and Mrs. Fang agreed to meet us at the mall. Carefully, Mom applied lipstick in front of the mirror. She always put on makeup when she went to the mall. Even before she could afford to buy lipstick at Walgreens, she'd cut open a beet and apply the juice to her lips.

In the car, I kept glancing over at her. She'd put on a little too much lipstick, and with her bouncy curls, she looked kind of like Ronald McDonald. Still, it was nice to see her so happy. When we got to the mall, she seemed downright thrilled to see her friends.

"Lao ban niang!" the friends greeted her, which translated to "wife of a boss" in Chinese. My mother blushed. I wondered if her new friends knew that she wasn't just a sit-there-and-do-nothing *lao ban niang* like Mrs. Yao. My mom had just cleaned two dozen rooms with her bare hands.

At the thought of Mrs. Yao, I drew a sharp breath. I thought of the way she looked at me the other day when she yanked Jason out of the motel room. Or a year ago, when she saw me and my mom here in this very mall. I poked my mother, wondering if she still remembered that. "Hey, do you remember how we used to come here carrying fake shopping bags?"

I said it in a warm and proud way. We'd come so far from the days when we used to walk around the mall carrying department store bags — that we filled with toilet paper to look like they were full of stuff we'd bought. But my mom's face flushed a deep red.

"What do you mean, fake shopping bags?" Mrs. Zhou asked.

Uh-oh. Did I say something I wasn't supposed to? "I mean, the bags were real. . . ." I muttered, trying to walk it back. "There just wasn't . . . you know, stuff inside."

My mom's new friends stared at us like we were moldy old

dishrags. Quickly, Mom muttered an excuse about how we had to get home and rushed me out of the store.

In the car, she didn't say a word. I kept peering over at her, hoping she'd at least let out a sigh. But she held on to all of her anger, the way Lupe held on to her secret at school. I could feel it fermenting and thickening inside her, like the stinky tofu sitting in our kitchen cabinet at home.

She finally erupted when we got back to the motel. "How could you *do* that to me?" she wailed.

I rushed to my father's side on the sofa, and he scrambled to his feet. "What happened?" he asked.

"She embarrassed me in front of my new friends!" Mom pointed at me. "She told them we used to carry fake shopping bags! And now they're probably never going to talk to me again!"

"Good!" I shouted back. "I hope they don't, and I'm not sorry I told them about your stupid shopping bags!" I blinked furiously, trying not to cry. I was sick of her pretending. I'd thought that now that we owned the motel, she would stop pretending. But she just found new things to pretend about!

Mom plunged her face in her hands, like she was too mad to even look at me. I looked to my dad but he just shook his head, so I got up and went to my room.

That night, the sounds of my parents arguing seeped through the thin walls. I hadn't heard them argue like that in a long time, not since we took over the motel. My dad accused my mom of losing her mind with me, to which my mom replied, "You're right. I am losing my mind. I'm not this! I don't care how much money we're making, I'm not a maid!"

Footsteps stormed through the manager's quarters and out the back.

"Where are you going?" I heard my dad say to her.

"I'm sleeping in one of the guest rooms tonight."

I cowered under the covers, wondering whether my words at the mall had cost a lot more than my mom's new friends.

CHAPTER 23

Light poured in from the window the next morning.

My eyes blinked open to see my dad sitting next to me on my bed.

"Where's Mom?" I asked.

I heard banging in the kitchen and immediately feared the worst. *She's moving out. She and my dad are getting a divorce. She's packing up her stinky tofu as we speak! I'm going to have to split weekends like poor Kenny Jacobson in the club.*

"She's just in the kitchen," he assured me. I felt my shoulder blades relax as my head sank back down on the pillow.

"Is she okay?" I asked, pulling the covers up to my chin.

My dad nodded. "Adults fight sometimes. I'm sure you and Lupe have disagreements too." That we did, usually about Jason. Dad reached out and gently touched the tip of my nose. "It doesn't mean you're not best friends."

I got out of bed, and together, we walked into the kitchen. My mom was in the kitchen drinking a cup of jasmine tea. She put down her cup when she saw me. Her eyes were swollen like she'd been up all night crying.

"I'm sorry," I said softly.

She shook her head, and for a second I worried that she wouldn't accept my apology. But then she said, "No, *I'm* sorry," and reached over to take my hand. She patted a spot on her leg, and I climbed into her lap like I did when we first got on the plane to fly to America, before the flight attendant told me I had to sit in my own seat. "I just wanted to be normal and have a night out," she confessed. "And feel what it's like to have a credit card like those ladies . . . and to have made it in this country."

I closed my eyes, breathing in her words and her lavender Pine-Sol smell.

"Oh, Mom," I said. "You're ten times better than those ladies."

She shook her head sadly. "They're probably never going to call me again. . . ." She sighed, glancing at the phone.

I gave her a hug, then got up to get the sesame oil. I knew just the thing to make her feel better, even more than shopping.

"How about a Mia Tang signature sesame oil shoulder rub?"

Finally, a smile escaped from my mother's lips.

• • •

Lupe came over the next day to help me at the desk while Hank went to volunteer at the ACLU. She was in an extra good mood because she said that her mom had found a coyote and was going to be on her way back soon.

"That's great!" I exclaimed.

I went out to the pool to do the weekly water pH test with the little strips my dad gave me, thinking about how we should throw a party for Lupe's mom when she got back. I was so distracted, I almost didn't notice the poster. It wasn't until I was bent down beside the water that it caught my eye. There, taped up on the wall, was a big handwritten sign with the words *Whites Only*.

I let out a piercing scream and dropped all the test strips. They flew everywhere, littering the blue water. I lunged for the poster and ripped it off the wall.

Who wrote this? Was it one of the customers? I scrunched to the ground, hugging my legs, my body shaking. I gazed up at the big sign: *Immigrants Welcome.* Did some racist nut see our *Immigrants Welcome* sign, sneak in here, and put up their own sign? Did someone I checked in at the front desk do it?

Lupe must have heard my scream, because in seconds she came running toward me, calling, "What's wrong? What happened?"

I opened up my hand to show her. Lupe's face clouded over like a storm when she saw the words *Whites Only.* She took the poster from me and crumpled it up.

"Don't be scared," she said, looking around the pool, eyes scanning for any other hateful posters. But it was just the one. "They want us to be scared," she added loudly, as if whoever wrote the poster might be hiding right in the bushes. "But we won't give them the satisfaction, will we, Mia?"

I shook my head. Lupe reached out and helped me up. Together, we walked back to the motel office, where we sat for the rest of the day, eyes glued to the front window, watching who came in and out of the pool like two hawks. I felt safe, having my best friend next to me. Still, the question blazed inside me: Who wrote this trash and put it up in our motel?

CHAPTER 24

After the horrid poster at the pool, everyone's spirits were in a slump. To take our mind off things, Hank and I embarked on a project—repainting the front office walls, which were peeling from years of neglect.

We went to Home Depot, where I picked out a sunny light yellow color. We lined the front office floor with newspaper, took all the frames and keys down from the walls, rolled up our pants, and started painting. When we were done, the office looked ten times brighter than before.

Still, our warm yellow walls did little to attract customers. It seemed like ever since the big *Immigrants Welcome* sign went up, cars drove right past us, turning into the Topaz Inn or the Lagoon Motel next door instead.

"You think it's the sign?" I asked Hank.

He shook his head and said, "If it is, we don't want their business anyway."

With less business, there was less money to go around. My mom sewed up holes in the sheets instead of ordering new linens, while my dad rummaged through the guests' trash, trying to find aluminum cans we could sell. But none of this was good enough for our paper investors. They started calling up at the beginning of October, asking about the lukewarm sales.

Mr. Cooper, one of our biggest paper investors, was particularly upset. "I don't understand," he barked over the phone one afternoon. "You guys had a great summer. Why's business down all of a sudden?"

It was a good question, one I'd been asking myself. We had a better location than the Topaz and the Lagoon. Why drive by us to go to them?

One day, I came home to a room full of angry-looking investors gathered in the manager's quarters. My parents poured tea while Hank and I tried to calm them down and assure them that business would pick up soon.

"How can you say that when you have a twenty-foot sign out front that offends people?" Mr. Cooper asked. "Don't you know we're in the middle of an election?"

Mr. Lewis held his hands up. "Listen, we got nothing against immigrants. But this is a *business*."

"Yes, and it has certain values," I reminded them. "Values you believed in back when we all bought the Calivista. Which is how we got here."

Mr. Cooper made a face, as if to say, *Values schmalues*. Funny how people change, four big, fat profit checks later. Mrs. Miller pursed her lips.

"Hank, you know what we're saying, right?" she asked. I looked over at Hank and at my parents, who wiggled uncomfortably in their seats.

I turned to the investors, crossed my arms, and said firmly, "Sorry, but we're not taking down the sign."

"In that case, I'd like to sell my shares," Mr. Cooper said. My dad's face went as white as a milk-soaked bedsheet. "I'd like my fifty thousand dollars back. I don't want to be one of the owners of the Calivista anymore."

"Now, just wait a minute," Hank started to say.

But Mr. Cooper reached for his briefcase and got up. "I'm sorry, but that's my decision," he said. He looked at me. "Mia, you know I like you, but this is business, not personal. I'm not going down with the *Titanic*."

The *Titanic*? What a thing to say! As I watched Mr. Cooper and the others leave, I put my head down on the front desk. I thought briefly of taking down the sign, but it was *our* motel. The investors weren't supposed to tell us how to run it. They were just paper investors — that was the deal.

The mailman knocked on the front door, and I buzzed him in. He handed me a bunch of letters, including a really thick one. It was from Visa, and it was addressed to my mom. I immediately sat up.

Dear Ying Tang,

We received your letter asking us to reevaluate our rejection of your credit card application, and on appeal, we're pleased to inform you we have decided to approve your application. Enclosed please find your new Visa credit card with a $300 limit.

Thank you for your patience and thank you for choosing Visa. We are honored you have decided to build your credit history with us.

Yours,

Visa Credit Card Customer Service

"MOM!" I cried.

Pasted below the letter was her shiny new credit card!

CHAPTER 25

My mom was overjoyed to get her new Visa card. And I went to school armed with a new word — appeal. Mrs. T said an appeal was like a do-over. In America, we didn't have to accept the first decision. We could ask a "higher body" — someone with more power — to reconsider. In my heart of hearts, I'd always thought it would work like that, but it was great to know there was an official word for it. I couldn't wait to tell all the other kids in our club!

Under the tall oak tree, I walked them through how they too could appeal their parents' rejections and denials. The other kids whooped with excitement, so loudly that one of the teachers on playground duty walked over to us.

"What's going on here?" Ms. Steincamp asked.

"Nothing."

"You're supposed to be playing!"

"We *are* playing," I insisted. But Ms. Steincamp shook her head, unconvinced.

"Fine, then, let's see you play," she said. She took off her sun hat, put her clipboard on the grass, and leaned against the tree, watching us. When it became clear she wasn't planning on leaving, the other kids got up, one by one, and walked away, until it was just me, Lupe, and Jason left. We sat there, confused, until the bell rang to go back to class.

When Lupe and I reached Mrs. Welch's room, Bethany Brett was screaming her head off. A cockroach the size of a small Snickers bar was sitting on her desk.

"Ahhhhh!!! Get it off!!!" Bethany pointed to the big bug, flailing her arms.

At the mention of the word *cockroach*, all my classmates started freaking out, leaping on the chairs and tables. You'd think they'd never seen a bug before. A bunch of the boys shrieked, and some were even *shivering*. Mrs. Welch grabbed a newspaper, and I thought she was going to kill it—but instead, she just used the paper to cover the books on her desk.

I rolled my eyes and made a mental note never to be stuck on a deserted island with any of them—except Lupe, who looked at me like, *Are you going to do it or am I?* I gave her a quick nod. With two swift moves, I took off my shoe and smacked that cockroach dead, as I had done a thousand times at the Calivista.

Everyone stared at me, too stunned to speak. When I held up my shoe, triumphantly displaying the dead cockroach on it, the class erupted in thunderous applause.

"That was *awesome*," Stuart said, grinning.

Bethany Brett, though, sneered at me. For someone who'd just had an enormous roach removed off her desk, you'd think she'd be a little more appreciative. But all she said was, "That's because she lives in a *roach* motel."

I turned toward her and waved the cockroach-covered shoe in the air.

"What did you say?" I asked.

The other kids cowered, shielding their eyes from the bloody pest.

"Don't ever call me Mia the maid again," I warned Bethany.

She swallowed hard and looked away. As I left to clean my shoe in the bathroom, I heard one of my other classmates whisper, "Did you see the way she *whacked* it?" I couldn't help smiling.

In the hall I bumped into Principal Evans. "Hey, Mia, what's up with the bloody shoe?" she asked. I quickly explained.

"Wow, and you got it off Bethany's desk? That's so brave of you. I'm sure Bethany is very appreciative," she said, smiling.

Yeah, right. I glanced over at my classroom, wondering whether I should bring it up with Principal Evans.

"What's wrong?"

I took a deep breath. "Principal Evans," I said, "I'm tired of the name-calling and the bullying around our school. And I'm not the only one. I know eighteen other kids who feel the same."

Principal Evans stared back at me. *"Really?"*

I nodded.

"Well, that is not acceptable," she said. "We at Dale Elementary take bullying very seriously. I'm going to have a word with the teachers and see what we can do about this."

Hope surged inside me.

"Is there something else?" she asked.

I hesitated. But since I had her attention, I knew I had to ask. "A bunch of kids and I, we like to talk during recess. By the tree. Is that okay?"

"I don't see anything wrong with that," Principal Evans said. With a wink, she nodded at my dripping shoe. "Now you better go get that cleaned up."

I practically skipped the rest of the way. Who knew a cockroach could make my day?

CHAPTER 26

The next morning at school I was watching Bethany Brett pour hand sanitizer all over the spot on her desk where the cockroach was, as though it had been permanently soiled, when the intercom crackled to life.

"Good morning, students of Dale Elementary School," Principal Evans's cheery voice said. "I have an exciting announcement to make. Next Friday, we're going to be holding a very special event. An event intended to bring us together as a community, while promoting the school values of kindness, care, and consideration."

I looked over at Lupe, who smiled back at me, wiggling in her seat.

"Are you guys ready?" Principal Evans asked. "We're going to have a . . . COOKOUT!"

I could almost hear Jason cheering from the next trailer. Principal Evans explained that it was going to be potluck style, with every family bringing a dish. All around me, my classmates started shouting out what they were going to bring — paella, chicken parm, hummus, fajitas, curry!

It all sounded delicious, but I had a feeling that the dish that was sure to knock everyone's socks off was whatever Jason was going to be cooking up.

"YESSSSSSS!!!" Jason yelled the second I saw him at recess. I laughed. We walked together to the big oak tree, Jason talking a mile a minute about all the things he wanted to make—braised pork belly with caramelized chili, shredded chicken salad with coconut, miso butterscotch ice cream for dessert. It made everyone's mouths water just hearing about it!

He got on his knees in front of the oak and thanked the school gods for the opportunity to show off his culinary prowess in front of his classmates. "You know how long I've been waiting for this?" he asked.

I giggled, then asked, "Is your mom going to come?" I thought back to the other day, when she jerked him away from me like I was a virus. Still, I knew she'd be proud of Jason.

But he shook his head. "She'll be away at this art thing in Las Vegas. She's trying to sell some of our paintings."

Sell their paintings? I raised an eyebrow but didn't say anything. Lupe just looked relieved that she wouldn't have to see Mrs. Yao. I had to admit I was too.

"But my dad might come!" Jason declared.

And . . . the relief disappeared. I couldn't believe I was going to have to have dinner with Mr. Yao *again*.

• • •

When I got home, I found Hank and my parents in the front office, celebrating their own good news.

"Guess what, Mia?" Hank asked. "The line of credit finally came through! We did it!"

I flung my backpack to the floor and joined hands with them, jumping up and down.

"That's *great!*" I exclaimed. "So now we can buy Mr. Cooper's shares from him?"

Hank chuckled. "Not quite," he said. "But it means we can take out a loan if things don't pick up, or if they get worse."

I glanced over at the big sign. I sure hoped business would pick up soon. Walking out of the manager's quarters, I noticed little pieces of blue paper peeking out from under the doors of the rooms. Puzzled, I reached down and picked one up. It was a flyer, and when I saw what was printed on it, the blood drained from my head.

The flyer had a picture of a machine gun blasting bullets into a dark-skinned man with the words *USA NOT USI: United States of America NOT United States of Immigrants* written across the top.

Shock and anger pulsed through my veins. I ran all the way back to the office and showed my parents and Hank. After the *Whites Only* sign, we'd all been upset. But this time, we called the police.

It took the police an hour and a half to finally get over to the motel, and by that time we had already grabbed all the flyers. They were underneath *every* guest room door, which the police said meant they couldn't have been made by a customer.

"How do you figure?" Hank asked. I could tell he was trying very hard to keep calm underneath his perfectly ironed white shirt. Cops made him nervous, and understandably so. Last year they'd wrongly accused him of stealing a guest's car.

The taller cop, Officer Ryan, said, "If it's a customer, he wouldn't put the flyer under his own door. But you guys said it was underneath everyone's door."

Hank and I exhaled in relief. It was good to know that our customers weren't behind something so hateful.

Officer Ryan looked up at our big *Immigrants Welcome* sign. "You thought about taking that down?" he asked.

I shook my head. "We're not going to take it down," I said to him firmly.

The other police officer shook his head. "Suit yourself. But you're just asking for trouble. The state is in a crisis. There are all sorts of angry people out there, and they're looking for targets to blame." He looked down at his notepad. "We had thirty-two complaints of hate speech this month alone. And it's not even close to Halloween."

I looked the officer right in the eyes and said, "We're not asking for trouble. We're asking for kindness."

CHAPTER 27

I didn't get much sleep that night. I was too upset after talking to the police, who, after all that talk, said they couldn't do anything to help us because the flyers were protected by free speech.

I was also worried about our customers. What if the next time a hateful sign or an awful flyer showed up, they saw it before we did?

The very next morning I found a handwritten note tucked under the front office door. I braced myself for more venom. But when I picked it up, the nicest words greeted me.

I just wanted to say, I noticed your sign. My grandparents came over to this country from Poland some 80 years ago. Thank you for making immigrants feel welcome.
—Mrs. Johnson (Janowicz originally, but got shortened to Johnson at Ellis Island), room 19

The words filled my heart with hope and I framed the note and put it up on our freshly painted yellow wall.

• • •

On Saturday, Uncle Zhang came over as my dad and I were about to leave for the library. Eagerly, I showed him Mrs. Johnson's note.

Uncle Zhang beamed and said he was proud of me, then turned to my dad and shared his own frame-worthy news.

"Guess what? I passed my electrical technician certification exam!"

"You're on the main road now, buddy!" my dad said, patting Uncle Zhang on the back. The "main road" was this thing my parents and their friends were always talking about. I didn't know where it was exactly, if it was even a real road, but I knew it was something good and preferable to the side streets, which we were on.

"I didn't think it would ever happen!" Uncle Zhang shook his head, still grinning.

My dad handed Uncle Zhang his envelope for that week, apologizing that it was a little smaller because business had been down. But unlike the paper investors, Uncle Zhang didn't freak out.

"Don't worry!" he said. "I'll help spread the word and drum up more customers. And once I start my new job, I'll be working with lots of *lao wai*, and I'll tell all my colleagues! I could put brochures at the doctor's office too. I'll be getting benefits with my new job!"

My dad looked down at his tattered pants. His face puckered, like he'd just drunk a bowl of vinegar. Uncle Zhang quickly added, "Hey, one of these days you'll be on the main road too, my friend. All you have to do is study—"

"No time," my dad replied, gazing over at the vacuum cleaner sitting in the corner. "Too busy cleaning."

After Uncle Zhang left, I asked my dad what this main road was. He chuckled and said, "The main road just means having a job that pays proper."

I looked around, almost wanting to protect the innocent ears of our fine new walls. "This job doesn't pay proper?" I asked.

My dad patted my head and playfully messed up my bowl-cut bangs. "You worry too much," he said. "Now, let's get you to the library. You said you wanted to borrow a cookbook this week?"

I nodded.

At the library, I browsed through the cookbooks, looking for a simple recipe to make for the school potluck, then wandered over to the History section to get a book on undocumented immigration.

As we were leaving, I noticed my dad had borrowed a few books of his own.

"What are those?" I asked.

He flushed, slightly embarrassed, and hugged the books tight. "Oh, these? Nothing." He tried to cover up the titles with his hands, but I could still read them on the spine: *English Made Easy* and *Lab Technician Certification Study Guide*. "I just thought I'd get them, you know, just in case."

I thought back to what he'd said about the main road. But if my parents switched jobs, who would clean the rooms every day? Who would leave an extra blanket in the guest rooms in the winter when it got cold? More importantly, who would greet me with a smile after school when I charged up the stairs to let them know I was home? Suddenly, I was seized with panic.

"Don't worry, my little penny," my dad said. "Thinking and doing are two very different things . . . sadly." He sighed as he checked out the books.

I looked up at him, wanting to ask, *What do you mean?* but also not wanting to ask. I just wanted to hug the relief that my dad wasn't going anywhere.

CHAPTER 28

At school the next week, all the kids were excited about the cook-out. But Lupe's mind was on something else.

"Guess what?" she whispered, bouncing next to my desk. "My mom's on her way back! She left with the coyote last night!"

"That's great!" I whispered back, throwing my arms around her to give her a hug.

Mrs. Welch cocked her head as she passed back our math quizzes from last week. Both Lupe and I had gotten an A this time. "Are you guys talking about the big debate on TV between Wilson and Brown last night?" she asked. "Did anyone see it?"

A few kids raised their hands.

"My dad says a woman can't be governor," Michael said. "That's a man's job."

"Yeah!" Stuart said. "Girls just aren't tough enough."

I scoffed. "Not tough enough? Who's the one who killed the roach?"

"Yeah, well, that was . . . that was . . ." Stuart stammered. "That was just because my dad wasn't here. If my dad had been here—"

"And who runs a motel?" I continued, cutting him off. Bethany opened her mouth, but I shot her a look so intense, she promptly closed it. "Every day I get up at six a.m., come to school, work at the front desk after school, do my homework, do my mom's math worksheets on top of my homework, and write updates or call our investors to let them know what's going on. Not tough enough? Please, give me a break."

The entire room was silent.

"Thanks for sharing, Mia, that's very impressive," Mrs. Welch said, looking not the least bit impressed.

But I didn't care. *I* was impressed, for I had finally worked up the nerve to not be ashamed of what I did, but to be *proud* of it, to own it. And that was something!

. . .

Mrs. Welch asked me to stay behind at the end of the day for "a quick chat" while everybody else packed up and went home. I thought she just wanted me to clean the classroom again, so I started picking up the markers. But she told me to put them back down.

"You know, Mia, it's one thing to be proud of your job, but you shouldn't make others feel uncomfortable or bad," she said with a frown. "Remember what Principal Evans said about kindness?"

She was reminding *me* about kindness? I wanted to burst out laughing.

"What's so funny?" she asked.

I pinched my lips, but a smile was impossible to hold back — and my words were too. "Well, no offense, Mrs. Welch, but you're always saying things about immigrants. . . ."

Mrs. Welch stared at me like I'd just accused her of bleaching her hair with toothpaste. "I didn't say anything! I merely said they should be kept in check! If only a small number were allowed into the country, people wouldn't be so mad at them!'"

I glanced over at Mrs. Welch's diploma next to her desk. I knew it was wrong, but seeing as she was already mad at me, I asked, "Is that like at universities, only a small number get to teach there?"

Mrs. Welch followed my gaze. "So you saw my degree," she said. She walked over to her diploma and positioned her desk chair so it was hidden from view again. Then she came and took a seat in the chair next to mine. It was too small for her, but she squeezed into it anyway.

"It's true that I have a PhD, and that I ought to be teaching at the university level," Mrs. Welch admitted. "But sometimes in life, we don't always get what we want."

You can say that again. I glanced out the window, wondering if I could go home now. But Mrs. Welch was not done.

She picked up an eraser from my table and started playing with it, as though she was erasing something imaginary. "I didn't think I'd end up here," she said. She closed her eyes for a second. "I thought I'd be in the front of a lecture hall, discussing Brontë and Faulkner in an auditorium full of students. Not kids, but *real students*. You know?"

I shook my head. No, I didn't know.

"And I'd be the cool professor, showing them movies and occasionally having class outside on the lawn."

"That sounds nice," I offered.

"It was nice, at first. But when it came time for faculty selection, they kept promoting the men." She looked at me, slightly embarrassed. "I can't believe I'm having this discussion with an eleven-year-old. You couldn't possibly know what it's like to be passed up for something, or not be able to do what you were meant to do."

"Actually," I said quietly, "my mom used to be an engineer in China, but now she cleans motel rooms. So I know a little about that."

Mrs. Welch didn't say anything, but I could tell from the look on her face that she did not expect to hear *that*. As I packed up my stuff to go home, Mrs. Welch didn't go back to her desk. She stayed right where she was, squished in the kid's chair, her eyes a river of thoughts.

CHAPTER 29

The school was decorated in red and white balloons, our school colors, on the day of the big cookout. Excitedly, I carried the aluminum pan full of my mom's fried rice and chicken chow mein across the field. My mom was carrying the stainless steel serving spoons that she'd bought with her new credit card. There were families everywhere, all holding hot pans of tasty food.

"Mia!" Jason called. He was in a chef's hat and apron and standing proudly in front of a table of deliciousness. I waved and walked over to where he was presenting three bowls of his roasted pork belly for me and my parents to taste. "Tell me this is not the best pork belly you've ever had!"

I took a bite. The meat, oozing with flavor, melted on my tongue. The kick of the caramelized chili balanced perfectly with the golden crispy skin. "This is the *BEST* pork belly I've ever had!" I declared, and my parents agreed.

"It better be," Mr. Yao's voice bellowed from behind us. "It cost $3.99 a pound! I tried to get him to make something cheaper—"

"Yeah, he wanted me to bring canned beans." Jason rolled his eyes.

"What's wrong with canned beans?" Mr. Yao protested. He looked over to my parents, who said hello. He pointed at the two of them and asked, "Who's watching the motel if you're both here?"

My parents immediately tensed, as though they were still working for him. Before they could answer, Mr. Yao declared, "You know what, it's not my problem anymore!"

Instead, he peered down at my mom's dish and asked her what we brought.

"Fried rice and chow mein," my mom said. "Would you like to have some?"

Mr. Yao clapped his hands together. "Now, that's my type of Chinese food!" he said, eying the dish like it owed him money. My mom chuckled and started serving some up for him with her new serving spoons.

As Mr. Yao wolfed down my mother's rice and mein, I skipped over to find Lupe. She was on the other side of the field with her dad. They were serving tamales, guacamole, and chips. I picked up a tamale, letting it cool in my hand.

"Can you believe this?" Lupe asked, pointing at all the banners and other decorations that the school made especially for the cookout. They said things like *Kindness matters!* and *What's free and priceless? Being nice!* "I wish my mom were here. She'd love this!"

I put my arm around Lupe's back, and we gazed across the field. The sunset had turned the sky into a canvas of colors. "When will you guys know if she's crossed back safely?" I asked.

"Hopefully in the next couple of days. She's in the desert as we speak."

I gave her a little squeeze, knowing how dangerous that trip could be. "She'll be back before you know it," I assured Lupe. "Hey, have you tried Jason's pork belly yet?"

Lupe shook her head and her body stiffened, but I pulled her hand. Finally, she let me drag her to the other side of the field.

There was a line a mile long in front of Jason's stand when we got there. Lupe got in line. At the front of the line, a couple of students I recognized from Jason's class reached for the pork.

"This is amazing!" they remarked, devouring their pork. They looked at Jason in awe, and he scooped up miso butterscotch ice cream for them for dessert. Even Mrs. Welch was there — standing in line for seconds!

"I don't normally like ethnic food," she said. "But I have to say, this pork belly is quite good!"

I giggled as I walked back over to my parents' table. I found Mr. Yao sitting behind it alone, still munching on the fried rice. My parents were walking around the field, tasting everyone's food.

"You know, you shouldn't just fill up on fried rice," I said to Mr. Yao, remembering one of my dad's all-you-can-eat-buffet rules. "You should try some of your son's delicious pork belly before it runs out."

He shook his head. "Nah. Too heavy for me. I like my food plain and simple."

I turned and pointed at Jason's crowded stand. "Look at that line! You're missing out! Jason's going to be an incredible chef one day."

"I hope not." Mr. Yao coughed, as though a grain of rice went down the wrong pipe. "He's got to advance, not go backward."

I furrowed my eyebrows. What was he talking about?

"Like your family," Mr. Yao said, waving his chopsticks at my parents on the other side of the field. "You used to be employees, and now you're owners."

He turned back to his rice with a melancholy sigh. And I stood there, very, very quiet, under the early evening moon. It was the first time Mr. Yao had ever let on that he was impressed with us. I didn't want to care what he thought of my family, but he was right. We'd come a long way.

CHAPTER 30

Lupe wiggled at her desk, staring at the clock. I knew she was counting the hours, and then the minutes, and then the seconds until school was over so she could run home and see if her mom was back.

At recess, I tried to distract Lupe by asking her what she wanted to be for Halloween. Last year, we all went as mummies. Hank thought it might be fun this year to go as Tetris blocks. We could make them out of the big empty boxes in the supplies room so that when we all lined up, we'd fit together.

"Tetris blocks works for me!" Lupe said.

Jason came hopping over. We were gathered underneath the tree, as usual. Thanks to the big kindness cookout and Principal Evans giving us her blessing to sit and talk at recess, our Kids for Kids club had grown even bigger — to twenty-two members! We couldn't even all fit underneath the shade anymore.

"Guess what the other kids are calling me now?" Jason asked. "Master chef!"

"That's great!" I said. That sounded *a lot* better than Chinese dough boy. "So are you going to talk to your dad about the cooking class?"

"No. . . ." Jason looked down at the grass. "He'd never go for it."

"What are you talking about?" I asked. I hated seeing Jason give up like that. "You saw it for yourself at the cookout. You're an amazing cook. Everybody knows it!"

All the other kids under the tree nodded. We took turns describing how good his food was.

"You make pork taste like . . . Doritos!" Hector said.

"You make eggs taste like marshmallows," I added, thinking back to how delicate and light and fluffy his eggs were.

Lupe threw out, "You make miso butterscotch ice cream taste like . . ." She paused and thought for a second. "Silk."

Jason looked at us all in surprise.

"You have a gift," I told him. "You have to do something with it."

Jason's eyes grew even wider. I couldn't believe it myself—just a year ago, Jason had been my nemesis. And now I was saying that he had a gift (and not for stealing pencils). But it felt good to encourage him to go for his dreams, even if his dad didn't think of them as "advancing." *Especially* when his dad didn't think of them as advancing.

CHAPTER 31

Lupe wasn't at school the next day, so I assumed her mom had come back safely and she was just taking the day off to spend some time catching up with her. In class, Mrs. Welch seemed more happy and content than usual. Perhaps the kindness posters, which were still up all around school, had rubbed off on her. After lunch, she put on some classical music and let us have a free write — no topic, no grades. We could write on anything we wanted.

I wrote a story about Lupe's mom crossing the hot desert. Then, just as our time was about up, I realized, *Oh, no, what if Mrs. Welch reads this?* Frantically, I started crossing everything out. When Mrs. Welch came to collect my journal, she stared down at my blacked-out pages and frowned.

Back at the motel, I found my mom and dad cleaning in room 10.

"How was business today?" I asked them.

"It was okay," Dad said. "Thank God for the immigrants. They're our most loyal customers now."

"Of course, we do give them a discount," my mom added, as she pushed the vacuum. They were cleaning without the air conditioner on to save money. Sweat collected in circles around my mom's armpits.

"Which means we make less," I thought out loud. "Too bad we don't have more rooms. . . ."

"We could rent out the lawn chairs by the pool!" my dad joked. My mom and I laughed.

My mom turned the vacuum off and sat down on the bed for a little rest. She pulled the scraps of math out of her pocket to study them.

Just then, we heard a scream from the parking lot.

"MIA!!!!!"

My mother jolted up, dropping her math scraps, and we both ran out of the room. Lupe was standing in the middle of the parking lot, her eyes red and swollen, her hair a disheveled mess. She was wearing the same shirt she'd worn the day before and tears gushed from her eyes. When she saw us, she ran over.

"My dad drove down to the border to try to find my mom, and they . . ." She struggled to get the words out. "They've taken my dad!"

My mom shook her head like she didn't understand. "Who's they?" she asked.

"The immigration police — they've got him!"

CHAPTER 32

Shaking, Lupe stood in the middle of the manager's quarters telling my parents, the weeklies, and me what happened. Her dad went down to the border to look for her mom, who still hadn't come back from Mexico. When he didn't come home, Lupe had a bad feeling. That afternoon, her worst nightmare was confirmed. Her dad called her from jail to let her know he'd been picked up by the immigration police.

Mrs. T handed Lupe tissues as she cried, hugging her in her warm mama-bear arms, while Hank paced back and forth in the living room.

"Where is he?" Hank asked.

"He said he was down in San Diego County Jail," Lupe said. Mrs. T ran her hands up and down Lupe's shivering arms, over and over, as Lupe wailed, "I wish my mami was here. . . ."

Hank grabbed his keys. "We're going down there right now," he said.

There was some argument over whether Lupe should go, given her status.

"What if they take Lupe too?" my mom said. "She should stay here."

But Lupe broke free of Mrs. T's arms and held on to Hank's

arms. "Please, please take me to see my dad," she begged.

It killed me to see her like this. I couldn't imagine what Lupe was feeling inside. And to think that José, our dear, wonderful José, was locked up in jail. It wasn't fair! There had to be something I could do.

"I'll go with you too," I said, slipping my hand into Lupe's.

My parents exchanged a worried look. "I don't think that's such a good idea," my dad said.

I looked up at them. "Why not? We have papers." I'd seen them myself in the bottom drawer of my mom's dresser, along with all our old photographs from China. The photos were faded by now, but still, I looked at them sometimes to remember my grandparents' faces.

"We weren't born here," my mom said. "They could throw us out anytime they want." She walked over and guarded me with both hands, as if some invisible force was threatening to take me from her. It made me think of what Jason once said—*Maybe you and Lupe are in the same boat, but not me.*

"It's okay," Hank said. "Mia doesn't have to go. We'll be fine. I'll say Lupe's my daughter." He turned to Lupe. "You'll be safe with me."

"I'm ready." Lupe nodded to Hank.

I hung on to my best friend's hand for just a second longer, before letting go.

CHAPTER 33

My heart was all pins and needles that night as I waited for Lupe and Hank to come home. To pass the time, I read the newspaper. In the Food section, I found an article about a chef named Philip Chiang who opened a famous Chinese restaurant in Beverly Hills where all the movie stars went to eat. I'd just reached for the scissors to cut the article out for Jason when a couple with a toddler walked into the front office.

"We saw the sign," the man said, smiling at me. They told me they were originally from India and they drove down from Oakland to take their little one to Disneyland.

I waved at their young son, envious he got to go to Disneyland. My eyes suddenly watered at the thought that maybe now Lupe and I wouldn't be able to go. Biting my lip, I told myself *stop it*, and handed the couple their registration forms and the key.

"Thank you for putting the sign up," the woman said. "It's good to know we're welcome."

I smiled at them, still feeling the lump in my throat. After they left, I dropped my head on my arms on the front desk, gazing out the window at the passing traffic. Where were Hank and Lupe at this exact moment? Were they at the San Diego County Jail yet?

It was ten o'clock by the time Hank and Lupe got back. I was already asleep, but I woke up when I heard Hank's car and ran outside. The weeklies came out of their rooms too, and Mrs. Q scooped Lupe into her arms.

"Thank God you're all right," Mrs. Q said, kissing the top of Lupe's head.

Billy Bob turned to Hank. "So what happened? Is José okay?"

Hank sighed. His eyes were sad and heavy. "He's been better," he finally said. "They're trying to get him to waive his right to a hearing. Sign a voluntary departure form."

"You told him not to, right?" Fred asked.

Hank nodded. "I told him not to sign anything, to sit tight and not lose hope. We're going to get him out. First thing tomorrow, we're going to start calling immigration lawyers."

"I've got my big immigration book from the library!" I told everyone.

"And first thing tomorrow, I'm going to start calling up lawyers from the Yellow Pages!" Lupe added.

Hank reached with his hand and patted Lupe on the back. "I'm so impressed with you, you know that?" he said. Then he turned to the rest of us. "You guys should have seen her. She was so strong."

My parents, still in their pajamas, put their arms around Lupe. "Brave girl," my mom said. "You're staying here with us tonight."

"We can move an extra bed into my room!" I suggested.

Lupe locked arms with me.

As my dad went to get the rollaway bed, my mom knelt down on the ground in front of Lupe so she could look into her eyes. "I promise," Mom said, "we will do everything we can to get your parents back."

. . .

Lupe and I lay awake that night, staring at my ceiling. Neither of us could sleep a wink.

"Oh, Mia, the jail was horrible," Lupe said in the dark. She turned and told me how there was barbed wire everywhere, windowless cells, and tiny visiting rooms where people scratched words onto the walls.

"What kind of words?" I asked.

"Free Jenny. Don't be sad. I love you, Dad," she told me, her voice rising and falling.

I wiped my eyes on my pillowcase.

"And you know the worst part?" she asked. "I couldn't even hug him. All I wanted was to give him a hug, but there was a big glass wall between us and I could only talk to him over the phone."

"We're going to get him out," I whispered, turning my wet pillow around.

She didn't say anything for a long time.

"Mia? I'm scared."

I looked over in the darkness. Slowly, I crawled out of my bed and went over to Lupe. The rollaway bed rattled as I hugged my best friend.

"It's okay," I said, snuggling her.

"I'm trying to be brave, but I'm scared."

A tear fell down Lupe's face and landed on my hand. I thought about all the times last year when she was so brave, explaining to me how things worked in America, encouraging me to hang on tight and not lose hope. Now it was my turn.

"It's okay to be scared," I said. "It doesn't mean you're not brave. Even the bravest people are scared sometimes." I wiped my eyes. "But you know what? We're going to get through this. Together."

"Thanks, Mia," Lupe answered, and gave my hand a tiny squeeze.

CHAPTER 34

I woke up the next morning to the sound of the fax machine beeping and phones ringing. Lupe's bed was empty. I jumped up and ran outside, where I found my best friend leading Hank, Billy Bob, and Mrs. Q in an immigration lawyer–finding mission at the front desk.

"Welcome to Operation Save José," Hank greeted me with a smile. "Would you like some breakfast?"

He pointed to the box of freshly baked croissants he'd picked up from the store. My mom came in and set down a fresh pot of tea next to them.

"No, thanks," I said, taking a seat next to Lupe and getting to work. I picked up an extra copy of the Yellow Pages and flipped to the *L* section for lawyer.

"We've been leaving messages for lawyers all over town," Lupe told me. She glanced at the clock. It was only 7:00. "Hopefully, when they open, they'll call us right back."

I got to work dialing and leaving messages. At a quarter to eight, Hank pointed to the clock and said to me and Lupe, "You guys better get to school!"

"Do we have to go?" I asked.

"Yes," Mrs. Q said. "But don't worry, girls. We'll carry on calling."

"C'mon, Mia," Lupe said, pulling me down from my stool. "We'd better go, while we still can."

I knew she meant it as a joke, but my heart lurched. In less than a month, the people of California were going to vote. I hoped they didn't vote to take away Lupe's education!

. . .

When we got to school, I handed Jason the article I had cut out about the chef.

"Thanks, but I'm not sure I want to go to cooking school anymore," he muttered, sticking the article in his pocket.

This was news. "Why not?"

Jason turned and gazed toward his classroom. "It's too expensive. My dad's businesses aren't doing well, I told you."

"C'mon, Jason, I'm sure there's a way — maybe they have a payment plan or something —"

Jason gritted his teeth and blurted out, "If you must know, my dad said cooking classes are for girls."

"That's the *dumbest* thing I've ever heard!" I sucked in a sharp breath, ready to tell him the million and one reasons why what his dad said was completely off base.

But before I could, Jason shrugged and said, "I don't know, maybe he's right." Then he turned and walked away.

I shook my head at his back. There's a Chinese phrase about "playing the piano to a cow." That's how I felt at that moment — like, what was the point? Jason was never going to change. It was as useful to try to persuade him as it was to play the piano to a cow. Maybe Lupe was right, I thought as I walked back. Maybe I'd just been wasting my time.

I tried not to think about Jason and his dad's ridiculous words for the rest of the day, which was hard because in class, the other kids were once again talking about Kathleen Brown.

"Did you guys see what she said on TV yesterday?" Stuart asked. "That she's going to be tough on crime?"

Oliver grunted. "Oh, please, she's not going to be tougher on crime than a *man*!" Then he pretended he had a big machine gun in his hands and started blasting us all, making firing noises with his mouth. I scooted away in my chair, feeling a little ill, while my classmates shrieked with delight.

"That's enough, Oliver!" Mrs. Welch scolded him.

Bethany Brett raised her hand. "My mom said Kathleen Brown looks way *too* tough," she said. "Like one of those ladies at the hardware store." She made a face.

I didn't understand how someone could look both too tough and not tough enough at the same time, but several of the boys nodded in agreement with Bethany, like it was the truest thing they'd ever heard.

When the recess bell rang, I sprang up from my seat, but Mrs. Welch called my name.

"Mia, can you stay behind for a minute?" she asked.

I looked longingly at Lupe as she went out the door and headed to the tree. When everyone had gone, Mrs. Welch walked over to me.

"I was reading your latest essay, Mia," she said, placing it upside down on my desk. I stared at my paper, trying to make out the grade on the other side and will it into being an A. "I think it needs A LOT of work, but there's promise in some parts."

I glanced up. Did she say promise? Mrs. Welch smiled. It was weird to see a smile on her face, like a scrunchie on a flamingo. Something that's not supposed to be there.

Cautiously, I lifted the paper.

Another C.

I frowned and flipped it back over, anger mounting in my chest. It was a trick. She'd gotten my hopes up just to dash them, with more force this time.

"Why'd you give me a C if you thought it was good?" I asked.

"I didn't say it was good. I said it had *potential* to be good," Mrs. Welch clarified.

Was she messing with me?

"I'm sorry I'm not one of those teachers who give out As like candy," she said. "If everyone got an A, it wouldn't mean anything."

No, it would mean a lot. And what's wrong with candy?

"But if you're willing to put in the work, it might be possible for you," she went on. Then she took a deep, pensive breath, like she was probably going to regret this next part, but said it anyway. "I'd be willing to work with you one-on-one. During recess."

I looked up at her, not sure what to think.

"Are you interested?" Mrs. Welch asked.

I didn't answer right away. On the one hand, I did want to get better at writing. On the other hand, I *loved* my recesses with the Kids for Kids club. I wasn't sure I was ready to give that up.

Mrs. Welch must have taken my hesitation to mean a no, because she turned away and said, "That's too bad."

She walked back to her desk with a look of sadness — not a whopping amount, but enough to make me think maybe this wasn't a joke. Maybe she really wanted to help me to become a better writer.

The question was . . . did I want it from her?

CHAPTER 35

"Hi, I'm calling in regard to José Garcia. My name is Andrew Delaney. I'm an attorney with the law offices of Taylor and Associates," said the voice on the answering machine when Lupe and I got back to the motel from school. "We received your voice message, and we'd be pleased to schedule a meeting to see how we can help. Please give me a call back."

Lupe and I leaped into the air. A real lawyer called us back! I scrambled out of the front office shouting, "Hank! Great news!"

We all piled into the car—me, Hank, Lupe, and Billy Bob—and headed over to the law firm in downtown Los Angeles to meet Mr. Delaney. Lupe sat in the back seat next to me, chewing on her fingers. By the time we arrived, she had practically eaten an entire nail.

"Garcia family?" the smiling blond receptionist greeted us when we got up to the seventeenth floor. She was holding a clipboard and her hair was thick and shiny, like Jason's pasta right after he drained it from the boiling pot. The thought of Jason's pasta made me frown, though, and I pushed him out of my head.

"That's us," Hank told the receptionist.

I reached for Lupe's hand, and together we followed the receptionist to a solid oak door that opened up into a big conference room.

After the receptionist left to get Mr. Delaney, Hank and I looked out the window at the *incredible* view. It was a clear autumn day, and I could see the snowcapped peaks of Mount San Antonio in the distance. Hank and Billy Bob took a seat in the soft leather executive chairs. There was a plateful of chocolate chip cookies in the middle of the table. I thought back fondly to the ones Hank and I made, but I was too nervous to eat. Billy Bob reached for a couple.

The door opened again, and we turned around to see a short, older white man in an expensive-looking suit. He stuck out his hand and introduced himself as Mr. Delaney, then took a seat. He turned to Billy Bob and asked, "So in your message, you said that José Garcia was taken by the police a couple of days ago."

"Yes, my father, José Garcia," Lupe said, sitting on the edge of her chair.

Mr. Delaney looked at Lupe.

"She an illegal?" Mr. Delaney asked Hank.

Lupe flushed.

"Lupe and her parents do not currently have papers," Hank explained. "Her father's down at the San Diego County Jail right now. They asked him if he wanted to sign a voluntary departure form, which I told him not to sign." He looked to Mr. Delaney. "He shouldn't sign that, right?"

Mr. Delaney put up a hand. "Let's not get ahead of ourselves, now. Before we discuss any further, I need you to sign a retainer."

"What's a retainer?" Lupe asked. She looked to Hank.

Mr. Delaney took a piece of paper out from his folder and slid it across the table. "A legal contract that allows me to represent you.

Before I can give you any legal advice, you'll need to pay for my services. You'll see I charge by the hour and my fees are listed on the page."

We crowded around Lupe's chair to take a look at the paper.

I gasped. "Three hundred dollars an *hour*?"

"Plus incidentals," Mr. Delaney said.

Hank narrowed his eyes. "What incidentals?"

"Photocopying, phone calls, delivery fees, parking if I need to go to the jail or courthouse," Mr. Delaney said.

Hank gawked at the lawyer. "You want to charge us for *parking*? On top of three hundred dollars an hour?"

Mr. Delaney ran a hand through his thick, white hair. "It's gonna be the same at any law firm you go to," he said flatly.

But Hank was having none of it. "What else are you gonna charge us for? The paper clips? How about when you have to go to the bathroom? You gonna charge us for the toilet paper too?"

Mr. Delaney crossed his arms and side-eyed Hank. "We're not the Red Cross. We don't work for free."

"But you haven't even heard the facts of the case!" I protested.

Lupe started talking fast. "My dad's been here for eight years. He's never gotten into any trouble with the police, not even a parking ticket —"

Mr. Delaney cut her off with a wave of his hand. "You'll need to sign this agreement first."

Hank stood up from his chair. "You know, I thought you immigration lawyers actually wanted to help people. But you're all about money like everyone else. Worse, you prey on the weak." Hank turned to Billy Bob, Lupe, and me. "C'mon, let's get out of here."

On our way out, Billy Bob turned to Mr. Delaney and added, "And by the way, your cookies are stale."

As we waited for the elevator, I said to Lupe, "We'll find another lawyer."

Hank and Billy Bob nodded. "Absolutely," Hank said.

Lupe nodded silently, staring at the black marble floor. I looked down at our reflection as a tear escaped her eye and landed between us.

CHAPTER 36

Mr. Cooper called again that Saturday, asking how business was and whether he could sell back his shares. I felt like barking at him, "We have bigger problems to worry about right now than your shares!"

Then Lupe wondered out loud, "Maybe I should sell *our* shares in the Calivista . . . to pay for the lawyer."

"*NO,*" I told her emphatically. "Your family worked way too hard for that investment money. No way am I going to let it go to greedy Mr. Delaney and his stale cookies. We'll figure out something else."

"Play the lotto?" Lupe suggested, looking over at Hank.

Hank cleared his throat. "There is the line of credit from the bank. . . ."

But Lupe shook her head. "That's for the motel. For all of us."

"You're a part of 'all of us,'" I said. A lump grew in my throat. "You and your mom and dad."

At the mention of her mom, Lupe looked out the window. We still didn't know where Mrs. Garcia was, and with every passing day, the worry hung lower and heavier on all of us, like a soaking wet towel.

"I should go home in case she calls," Lupe said softly.

My mom walked over with a cup of cocoa. "I can't send you home alone. Stay here, with us."

"But what if she tries—" Lupe started.

"She'll know to try you here," my mom promised.

Lupe blinked back tears. "What if—what if something happened to her? The coyote won't know the motel's number."

Suddenly, I found it hard to breathe. I tried to shake the thought. "Nothing's happened to your mom. She's just taking a little longer to get back," I said to Lupe.

My dad drove Lupe home to get more of her clothes, and I sat at the desk, brainstorming ways we could track her mom down. Calling the police was out of the question because of her mom's status. But—maybe we could make a flyer for her? Maybe if we passed it out to some of the immigrants who came by, they might know someone who'd seen her or could get in touch with her coyote. It was worth a try.

The midday sun was streaming through the windows when Lupe got back. She liked the flyer idea and handed me a picture of her mom from her wallet, which we enlarged using the fax machine. First thing tomorrow, we would start handing out flyers to anyone and everyone who came through the motel!

That night, as we lay in bed, I thought about Mr. Delaney. What was so different about him that he got to make $300 an hour and my parents made less than $100 a day? It wasn't like he had an extra hand or a second brain—why was his time worth so much more than ours? Just because he could write and speak better English? I thought of Mrs. Welch's offer again. I flipped to my side and told Lupe about it.

"Maybe you should take her up on it," Lupe said. "My math got a lot better once your mom started working with me."

"But this is *Mrs. Welch* we're talking about. And what about the club?" I asked. "Besides, she doesn't even like my writing. She's not like Mrs. Douglas."

Lupe yawned in the dark. "You know, I won an essay contest too, once."

I propped myself up with my pillow. "Really?"

"Yeah. The topic was *What do you want to be when you grow up?* I wrote about wanting to be an artist and drawing trees so majestic, they looked like castles."

I smiled. "Why *are* you always drawing trees?" I asked.

"My mom says people — our family — we're like the trees. If we set our roots deep enough, we can't be moved."

It was such a beautiful image that I reached out in the dark for her hand.

We were going to put her family back together. In the morning we'd call up more lawyers and start passing out the flyers. Maybe I could even call up Annie the reporter and ask her if she had any ideas. Whatever it took, we weren't going to give up until we got them back together again.

As we held hands in the moonlight, I asked Lupe, "So what happened with the essay contest?"

She exhaled heavily, staring up at the cobwebs on the ceiling. Even though my parents were professional cleaners, our own rooms were always full of cobwebs. I guess they were too busy cleaning . . . to clean.

"I worked hard on it, putting in similes like we'd learned about in class," Lupe said to the cobwebs.

I nodded. Mrs. Welch was big on similes too.

"Two weeks later, we got a phone call from the district. Out of all the third grade stories, they picked mine. They were going to send it to the state contest."

I sat up in bed. "That's amazing!"

Something about Lupe's long pause, though, told me this was not the kind of story with a happy ending. She let go of my hand, and I lay back down, biting the soft corner of my blanket as she continued.

"The next week, the state essay people called. They wanted more information, like my birthday, my social security number. They said the contest came with a cash prize."

"That's great!"

Lupe shook her head. "No, it wasn't. They wanted to know our bank account information . . . and that's when my parents hung up."

"Oh, Lupe," I gasped in the dark.

She told me that at the end-of-year assembly, another girl got called up to the front. They gave her Lupe's certificate.

"I'm so sorry," I whispered.

I thought about Lupe's words for a long time, thinking of how different and similar the two of us were. We were both girls with big hopes and dreams. But because of one piece of paper, we were on two different sides of the law. I didn't really understand before what that paper meant. But now, I was starting to realize, it meant the difference between living in freedom and living in fear.

CHAPTER 37

On Monday morning, I left a message for Annie at the newspaper, asking about coyotes and how to track a person who might be missing.

"Mia, Lupe, hurry, you're going to be late for school," my mom called as I hung up.

I swung my backpack on and handed my mom the two dozen flyers Lupe and I had made.

"Be sure to hand them out to every customer who walks in," I said.

Mom nodded and handed me two boxes of Pocky sticks in return. Hank was taking me and Lupe to San Diego after school to visit José. I'd finally convinced my parents to let me go. It was going to be about an hour and a half in the car each way and the Pocky was in case we got hungry.

At school, Jason walked up to me on the field. With his hands in his pockets, he said, "Thanks for the article."

I nodded. I didn't need him to thank me. I needed him to see that the world was bigger than the one his dad saw.

"You're right. I should just talk to my parents," Jason went on. Then he sighed. "But I already know what they're gonna say. They're just gonna say no. . . ."

I shook my head at him. "If you think that way —"

"You don't understand, Mia. I'm not like you!" he exploded. "You have nothing to lose. My parents want me to be a lawyer or a doctor! They have high hopes for me!"

His words burned. "And mine don't?" I snapped.

Jason's face flushed. Neither of us said anything for a long time.

Then I decided to let him in on a secret.

"I was exactly like you once, you know."

"Like me how?" Jason asked.

I gazed at the other kids lining up for class across the field, debating whether I should tell him. "I didn't think I could be a writer because of something my mom said. . . ." I muttered. "She said because English is not my first language, I was a bike and the other kids were cars."

I didn't know why I was telling him this, why I was letting Jason in on the most vulnerable part of me, but as I said the words and looked into his eyes, I felt a gigantic wall come down between us.

"Oh my God," Jason said, shaking his head furiously. "That is *so* not true!"

My eyes flashed with surprise at his strong response. "Thanks. But at the time, I almost believed her."

"And now?" Jason asked.

I drew a deep breath. I wished I could tell him now I knew for *sure* that I could be a writer, but the truth was, I still didn't. There weren't exactly any Asian American writers being profiled in the papers. But just because I couldn't see it, didn't mean I couldn't be it, right?

I stood up as tall as I could and told Jason, "Now I don't care what my mom or anyone says. It's my dream and nobody can take it away."

I said the words with all my courage and all my heart, and Jason peered back at me, the morning sun smiling in his eyes.

As I sat in class, I thought about my own words. If I expected Jason to get serious about his dream, I needed to put my pride aside and get serious about my own. I knew what I had to do. At recess, while everyone else went out to play, I lingered behind and walked up to Mrs. Welch.

"I'd like to take you up on your offer," I told her. "But on one condition."

Mrs. Welch raised an eyebrow.

"My friends and I, we have a club. It's called Kids for Kids. And we'd really like it if we could have a room to meet in during lunch," I said.

Mrs. Welch put a finger to her chin, thinking. "I'll see what I can do," she said. She then walked over to the board and picked up the marker. "Now then, let's start with the basics. Mia, have you ever formally learned English grammar?"

I shook my head again. Not *formally*, no. I'd mostly picked up grammar from hearing the way the customers talked and from watching old reruns of *I Love Lucy*. Every time Lucy corrected Ricky's grammar, which was *a lot*, I took note.

Mrs. Welch jotted down the words *noun*, *verb*, *pronoun*, *adjective*, *adverb*, *preposition*, and *conjunction* on the board.

I opened my notebook and copied down the words. As Mrs. Welch explained what they all meant and the role they each played in a sentence, I tried to keep the rules straight in my head. It was a lot harder than watching *I Love Lucy*, and after about twenty minutes, my head started throbbing. I closed the notebook and rubbed my temples.

"Look, I know it's hard," she said. "Stay with me."

"Can we just write something?" I asked Mrs. Welch, turning to a blank page. "A story? An essay? Why do I have to learn grammar rules?"

"Because if you don't know the actual rules, you'll always be guessing," she said matter-of-factly. "You won't ever be sure."

I blew at my messy bangs. Mrs. Welch put her marker down and walked over to me. Once again, she squished herself into the small chair next to mine. "Hey. Don't you want to learn this stuff?"

I nodded, a slow and sad little nod, the kind that my mom usually gives my dad when he asks her if she wants to help him clean another couple of rooms after dinner. *How about it, whaddaya say?*

Mrs. Welch took a breath. "You know what writing is?" she asked. "Writing is half emotion and half technique. Right now, you have the first half, but you don't have the second half. And that's a shame because your first half is so *good*."

I was so shocked by the compliment, I looked around the room to make sure she was referring to me.

"The good news is, you can learn the second half," she said. "But it's very hard to learn the first half." She dropped her voice then and confessed, "It's something I never had as a writer."

I peered at her. "You never had any emotion, Mrs. Welch?"

She blushed. "I mean I *have* it, but not the way you have it," she said. "Like in your essay about the pizza deliveryman who skidded on the road, racing because he had to support his dying mother-in-law in Mexico. There's so much feeling there," Mrs. Welch said. "Did this actually happen to someone you know?"

I nodded slowly. *Yeah . . . and now he's in jail.*

"See, I don't usually get to see that colorful side to life," she admitted. "My life's so . . . you know . . . *normal.*"

Wow. It was the first time I heard anyone use *normal* like it was a bad thing.

"You should come to the Calivista sometime," I offered. I put my fingers to my lips as soon as I said the words. Did I just say what I think I did? But it was too late to take it back.

Mrs. Welch's pupils flashed. Now *she* looked around the room, as if I might be inviting someone else.

"Wednesdays are good," I added, and she smiled.

CHAPTER 38

On the way down to San Diego, Lupe muttered nervously, "I hope my dad's okay." She turned to me and added, "There are all kinds of *real* criminals in there with him!"

I squeezed Lupe's hand tight as Hank drove. When we arrived at the jail, I looked out to see a dark building with barbed wire around it. It looked . . . like a cage. My breath caught in my throat.

Hank led the way to the visitors' entrance and introduced himself to the attendant. He showed her his ID. He told her we were his daughters, and the attendant looked at him kind of funny, like, *Really? You have a Mexican and a Chinese daughter?*

"I like to keep it real," Hank said, by way of explanation.

The attendant shrugged and buzzed us in. Lupe and I pulled the hoodies of our sweatshirts up to hide our faces, as my parents had instructed us, so the surveillance cameras couldn't make us out on tape. As we walked through the double titanium doors, I peeked inside at the cells.

I saw prisoners lined up wearing orange jumpsuits. One guy saw us and started walking toward us. He was bald like Mr. Yao, but his skull was not smooth. Instead, it was all wrinkled and uneven, like he was wearing his brain on the outside of his head. Another guy had tattoos all up and down his arms and torso, even on his neck! I grimaced, thinking how much that must have hurt when he got them. These were tough street guys, nothing like our sweet, kind José. He was so gentle, if there was a squirrel up on the roof, he'd wait until it came down before going up to fix the cable.

The guard put us inside one of the visitation rooms, if it could even be called a room. It looked more like a library cubicle with a big glass wall and a phone.

As we waited, I traced my hand along the messages on the wall. They were just like Lupe described—heartbreaking, written by kids whose parents had been taken.

My dad's still #1.

Don't be sad.

And:

Mama come home.

Then there was a loud buzz, and the door on the other side of the glass swung open. José walked in, except he didn't look like José. He looked like a shell of José. He was so pale and skinny, like he hadn't eaten in days. His cheeks were sunken, and he had great big bags under his eyes.

"Papi!" Lupe called out to him.

She put her hand on the partition, and José put his on the other side, so their two hands met on the glass in the middle.

Lupe picked up the phone and started talking to her dad in a mixture of Spanish and English. She smiled through her tears at the sound of her dad's voice. As he talked, though, her face started falling.

"He said some of the other Latinos have been in here for

months," Lupe told us. "That's months without seeing daylight. Some of them say they hear voices."

I touched Hank's arm.

"He's asking again if he should just sign the voluntary departure form." Lupe looked into Hank's eyes.

Hank took the phone from her. "Do *not* sign those papers, my friend," he instructed José. "We are working on getting you a lawyer."

José shook his head. "How much is that going to cost?"

"Don't worry about that," Hank said firmly. But José kept shaking his head, like he was very worried about it.

I took the phone from Hank. "Hey, José, remember what you said to me? About not giving up?" I asked. "How everyone would say to you, *No can do*, but you didn't listen to them and you kept going?"

He mustered a small smile, but I could tell his spirit was fading. The time in jail was breaking him down.

"Papi, please!" Lupe begged him. "Have faith. Just hang on a little longer."

The warden came into the room and announced, "Time's up." José looked longingly at us as the warden pulled him out by the arm, and Lupe called out to her dad one last time.

"Hang on," she shouted through the glass. "For me, Papi. Please."

CHAPTER 39

The image of José's hand on the glass divider and Lupe's hand on the other side stayed with me the rest of the day. I kept imagining that it was my own dad in there and I might never see him again. No more Lucky Penny search nights. No more long drives out to Monterey Park. It made me wish I had eaten all the red bean shaved ice and always used chopsticks, even when I was eating cereal.

Lupe was quiet on the ride back. I guessed she was thinking about how we were going to get her dad out, and about her mom. She couldn't still be out in the desert. Had she been captured and put in one of these jails too?

When we got back to the motel, even before Hank turned the motor off, I jumped out of the car and ran to my parents to give them a great big hug. I clung to them for a long, long time, before finally letting go.

"How was he?" my dad asked.

Lupe shook her head. My mom pulled Lupe into her arms.

"Not great," Hank said. "He's losing his mind in there. We've got to get him out."

Lupe nodded, dabbing her eyes with her shirt sleeve, and headed back into the front office to make more calls. As she dialed attorneys' offices, I called Annie again to see if she had any leads on Lupe's mom.

"I'll definitely let you know if I hear anything through the news-wire," Annie said. "Do you know the coyote she was with? We've heard some cases of bad coyotes."

"Bad coyotes?" I gasped. I pictured conniving wolves with twitchy ears tying up Lupe's mom and going through her purse.

Annie added quickly, "I'm not saying that's what happened here."

But the fear had burrowed into me. "We've got to find her! Her husband is in jail. Her daughter needs her!"

I explained the situation with José. Annie asked if we'd started a petition.

"Would that help?" I asked.

"Oh, yes, it can be very helpful at the hearing, if you have something you can present to the judge. It shows that there's community support for José's staying."

I scribbled the words *START A PETITION* on my notepad. "On it!" I told Annie.

On Wednesday afternoon, as Lupe and I were working on the petition after school, someone walked into the front office. Someone we never thought in a million years we'd ever see at the Calivista.

"Mrs. Welch! What are you doing here?" I asked.

Mrs. Welch took off her light red jacket and hung it over her arm as she glanced around the front office. "You said to come by on a Wednesday," she said, clutching her purse tightly. She looked nervous.

"Right," I said. I got down from my stool and lifted the divider of the front desk. "Let me show you around."

I reached for the master key and took her out back to where all the rooms were. I grabbed two cream sodas from the vending machine as we passed by. I handed one to Mrs. Welch. As Mrs. Welch took a sip, she pointed at the congregation of immigrants outside Mrs. T's room.

"What's happening over there?" she asked.

"Oh! Those are the immigrants, they're here for Mrs. T's class," I said. I explained about the How to Navigate America lessons and walked her over, introducing her to everyone. There were five students that day, and they each smiled as Mrs. Welch shook hands with them, asking them what they did.

"I used to be a surgeon back in Bangladesh," one told her. "Here, I drive a taxi."

A woman from Mexico, Mrs. Morales, said, "I used to be a nurse. Here, I work at a massage parlor, giving foot massages."

"Really?" Mrs. Welch asked, surprised. "You were a nurse back in Mexico?"

"Sí," Mrs. Morales said.

"So why do you do this?" Mrs. Welch asked her, curiously. "Why come here to give foot massages?"

Mrs. Morales pointed to a five-year-old girl sitting in my mom's math class. "So my daughter can have a brighter future."

I stood with Mrs. Welch in the doorway, watching Mrs. T and Mrs. Q's class, as their students diligently copied down every word. I'd never seen my teacher so riveted, not even the time when she let us watch TV in class and Wilson announced he was cutting welfare.

Before she left, Mrs. Welch popped in on my mom's math class. Mom was so surprised to see my teacher standing there, she nearly dropped her new graphing calculator.

"Your daughter's a good student," Mrs. Welch said to her, shaking my mom's hand. "She has a lot of potential."

I couldn't believe my ears. Did I hear that right?

"Thank you." My mom smiled.

"I hear you used to be an engineer in China," Mrs. Welch said.

Mom blushed. "Yes. I used to make telephone systems."

"And now you teach math," Mrs. Welch said, pointing to the class.

"Only on Wednesdays," Mom said with a small laugh. "The other days, I clean the rooms."

Mrs. Welch nodded, as though she knew just the feeling. "We can't always do what we want." She looked over at me. "But we can try to make the best of what we do."

"Yes, we can," my mom agreed.

Lupe walked in to join us, and Mrs. Welch turned to talk to her. My mom put her arm in mine and led me over to a quiet corner, while her math students worked on a worksheet she'd designed for them.

"I'm proud of you, Mia. I know how hard it was for you at the beginning of the year. But you stuck with it."

Mom squeezed my arm, and my eyes crinkled. I was proud too.

CHAPTER 40

There were five messages on the machine when we got back to the desk, all from lawyers. The first four were from big law firms, and Lupe and I skipped right past those. The fifth one was from a lady named Prisha Patel.

"I'm an immigration lawyer in Buena Park. I'd be happy to sit down with you and talk about your case. My fees are reasonable, and the first consultation is free," she said.

The *free* part got our attention. I immediately called Ms. Patel back and told her we would come and see her tomorrow, right after school.

. . .

At our first Kids for Kids lunch meeting in the new trailer classroom Mrs. Welch got us the next day, Lupe and I passed around the petition for everyone to sign. Lupe had decorated it with tree branches that went all up and down the sides of the page like curvy ribbons. It was a petition to *FREE JOSÉ*.

Bravely, Lupe stood in front of the room. As she explained her dad's situation, tears rolled down some of the other kids' faces. I was so proud of Lupe, for getting up there and finding the courage to finally tell the other kids what she was going through. That day, every single member of Kids for Kids signed the petition, and several took extra copies so they could collect more signatures at home.

After the meeting, Jason handed me a little card. It was from the Orange County Kids Culinary Academy and read *Jason Yao, Future Chef*.

I grinned. "Your father's letting you go?"

Jason nodded, beaming. "It wasn't easy," he said. He leaned in closer so none of the other kids could hear. "Money's been really tight. We might even have to move houses soon."

I blinked in surprise. I had no idea things were *that* bad—but then I remembered the first day of school, when Jason said he hadn't gone anywhere over the summer, and then later at his house when he said his dad's businesses were down. I guess he'd been trying and trying to tell me, but I hadn't been very good at listening.

"How'd you talk them into it?" I asked.

"I told them just what you said. It's my dream and nobody can take it away." Jason crossed his arms and put on his *ain't taking no for an answer* face. I smiled. "Plus, you were right," he added. "There was a payment plan."

As the bell rang, I threw my arms around Jason and gave him a hug. I was so proud of him. He looked completely taken aback by my hug, as did Lupe, who turned away as soon as I glanced over at her.

"You have to come over to the motel to show me the new recipes you learn," I said to Jason.

"Sure thing!"

As the bell rang, Lupe walked over to me. "What was that?" she asked.

"Jason got into culinary school!"

"Oh, good, so he's moving schools?"

"No," I said, confused. "It's an after-school thing."

"Oh," she said.

I lifted an eyebrow. What was up with those two?

. . .

In class, all the kids were talking about the big march coming up against Prop 187 in downtown Los Angeles. The news had said that seventy thousand people were going to march! Mrs. Welch asked if any of us were planning to attend.

I looked around the room. No hands went up.

"Well, I do think it's important for us all to be informed," she said. "The state is about to make a big decision." She paused. I noticed she wasn't wearing her Pete Wilson button. "And there are a lot of good reasons on both sides."

Whoa. I glanced over at Lupe—her eyebrows were up too. I bounced in my seat, feeling a flicker of hope. Maybe this thing wasn't going to pass after all!

. . .

A smile played at my lips as Hank drove us over to Ms. Patel's office after school. I thought about what Mrs. Welch had said. I liked to think that I had something to do with it, though more likely she was just saying it to seem "balanced." Still, it was nice.

Lupe and Mrs. T sat beside me in the car. As Hank pulled into a strip mall, I furrowed my eyebrows. The lawyer's office was in a strip mall?

It took a while to find it, but we finally did, way in the back, nestled between a deli and a Foot Locker. Hank pushed open the rusty door. Inside were a desk, a couple of foldable chairs, a photo-copier, and a plant hanging from the ceiling that looked like it hadn't been watered in weeks. *Man.* It sure wasn't Mr. Delaney's fancy firm downtown.

The woman behind the desk swirled in her chair to face us. "Can I help you?" she asked.

"Uh . . . yeah . . . we're looking for Ms. Patel?" I said.

"That's me, Prisha Patel, sole practitioner," she announced. She got up and shook our hands. Ms. Patel was an Indian woman with silvery black hair, a warm smile, and glasses. She pointed to the plastic chairs in front of her desk. They looked like the chairs we had out by the pool. There were only two, so Lupe and Hank sat while Mrs. T and I stood.

Lupe got straight to it. "My parents and I are illegal aliens—" she said.

Ms. Patel held up a hand. "I'm going to stop you right there."

Oh, no, I thought. *Here we go with the retainer again.*

But that's not what she was getting at. "Actions are illegal, not people," she corrected.

"Excuse me?" Lupe asked.

"*Actions* are illegal, not people," Ms. Patel repeated. "And please don't call yourself an alien. Do you have green ears and a finger that can light up?" She got up again, smiling, and pretended to examine Lupe's ears.

"No," Lupe said, letting out a chuckle.

"Good. Then you're not an alien," Ms. Patel said.

Lupe glanced at me. I could tell she was thinking the same thing—*I like this Ms. Patel!*

The lawyer pulled out a legal pad and sat back down at her desk. "Let's get down to business. When did your father cross over?" she asked.

As Lupe gave her the dates and the details of how exactly her parents emigrated, I thought about our own journey to the United States.

My dad was a geneticist in China. A geneticist is a scientist who knows a lot about genes (*not* to be confused with jeans, which my dad knows nothing about). His friend in America wanted him to come work for him. He was starting a new biotech company, and he needed his help. My dad said he wasn't sure. His English wasn't great. But his friend insisted that good English wasn't necessary, only good skills. So my dad came and the company helped him with his immigration paperwork, putting him on the fast track to getting a green card.

But then the company went under. My dad's friend fled back to China.

My dad suddenly had no job, no money, poor English, and no one to turn to. He thought about going back to China, but he'd already quit his job, and he wasn't sure if he could get it back, even if he went begging to his boss. And he didn't want to go begging, couldn't stand the thought of his colleagues making fun of him for "not making it in America."

So we stayed. Yes, we had the green card. But we couldn't eat a green card for dinner. When the last of our savings dried up, my mom and dad started applying for manual labor jobs, and that's how we ended up at the Calivista.

I used to think it was pretty rotten luck, but now, listening to

Lupe describe how she and her parents had walked for days in the desert; how it got so cold they'd had to huddle together, skin to skin; how her father caught the rain with his hands and fed it to her — I felt grateful for my family's luck. Lupe's parents walked until the rubber soles of their shoes were completely rubbed off, until the blisters on their feet sprouted flowers. Still, they kept walking, their achy legs and empty stomachs fueled only by hope — the hope of better opportunity and safer streets for their daughter.

My parents and I flew here on a plane. There were no blisters. And I'd still had a scared flutter in my heart, not knowing what tomorrow would bring. Whether I was going to like my new home. Whether it was going to like me back. Even now, I could feel the flutter sometimes, like that day I'd found the awful poster at our pool.

Ms. Patel took notes as Lupe spoke, stopping at times to ask for locations, dates, and other details.

"And where's Mom?" she asked.

Lupe's voice wobbled as she told the lawyer she didn't know. She was supposed to cross back in the middle of October, and now it was a less than a week before Halloween.

I reached into my backpack and pulled out one of my flyers with Lupe's mom's picture on it. "We've been handing these out," I told her.

"Good," she said, taking the flyer from me and putting it on her desk. "If you manage to get in contact with her, tell her to stay put in Mexico, at least until your dad's trial is over."

"So you think there's hope?" Hank asked her. "You can get Lupe's dad out?"

"I'll do my best," Ms. Patel replied.

Lupe took a deep breath. "And what about . . . your fee?" she asked.

"We'll work something out," Ms. Patel said casually.

I shook my head. I'd been around the block long enough to know that *we'll work it out* meant we could be taken for a ride.

"We need to decide on it before you start," I told her. "We have some tip money from the summer saved up." I glanced at Lupe, who nodded eagerly. "Almost a hundred dollars!"

Ms. Patel chuckled and shook her head. "You know what? I'm going do this one pro bono. I'm the daughter of immigrants, so I know how it feels."

I looked over at Hank. He had a huge smile on his face.

"What's pro bono?" I asked.

"Pro bono is when you take on a case for free," Ms. Patel said. "Lawyers do that sometimes, if they find something worth fighting for. I'm sure you guys have let guests stay at the motel for free before?"

"Oh, have we ever!" I smiled.

Ms. Patel turned to Lupe. "Well, I think reuniting you with your parents is well worth fighting for," she said with a nod. "Don't you think?"

Lupe's chin quivered as she nodded back. As Hank shook Ms. Patel's hand and Mrs. T told her how grateful we were, I asked her if there was anything we could do to help.

Ms. Patel thought for a minute.

"I'd start talking to your neighbors, rallying up support. The more community support we have, the stronger our case will be."

Lupe and I grinned and proudly pulled out our petition to show her, with all the Kids for Kids signatures on it.

"Smart girls!" Ms. Patel said. "This is an excellent start. If you can get some more signatures, and perhaps even get some politicians or the media on our side, even better!"

We walked out of that tiny office armed with hope, determination, and the unbelievable luck that we'd found someone who believed in José's case as much as we did. It felt so good to know that the spirit of helping others lived not just in our sign, but in people's hearts too.

CHAPTER 41

As soon as we got back to the Calivista, Lupe went into our room, put her head down, and sobbed. It was like she was finally letting out all the tears she'd been desperately hanging on to. My mom said to leave her alone for a minute and brought me to the kitchen to help make some hot cocoa. When it was ready, we carried it back to Lupe.

"Is it your mom?" I asked her. "Are you missing her?"

Lupe sat up and took a sip of the cocoa. "I always thought . . ." she said, wiping her tears. "That because my parents did something illegal, that we were illegal, just like the bombs and the drugs. That we were bad. Today was the first time I heard someone official tell me I wasn't bad."

"Oh, Lupe," my mom said, sitting down next to her on the bed. She looked into Lupe's eyes. "Do you know how amazing you are? How smart and talented and incredibly gifted?" She took Lupe's hands into hers and interlaced her long fingers with hers. "These hands are the hands of an artist and a mathematician."

"And a writer," I added.

Lupe managed a small smile.

"And a motel owner," I continued. "And a translator!"

My dad walked into the room and chimed in, "Someone who makes the best guac and chips!"

Lupe giggled.

"Protector of immigrants!" I threw in. We were on a roll!

"People checker-iner!"

"Explainer of what's what!"

My mother hugged her. "A girl who bravely crossed into the unknown when she was a baby," she said.

"And the bestest best friend I am proud to have," I finished with a hug.

Lupe hugged me back, laughing and crying at the same time. "You guys," she said, putting a hand over her heart.

My mom kissed the top of Lupe's head as she walked out of the room. "Get your homework done before dinner, girls," she said to us. "I'm going to cook Lupe's favorite — sweet and sour chicken!"

My belly rumbled in eager anticipation. We had gone straight from school to Ms. Patel's office, and I was famished. As my mom left to go make dinner, I turned to Lupe, and because she was still looking a little sad, I suggested something crazy. When I whispered it to her, Lupe grinned.

After dinner, we waited until my parents were both asleep before sneaking out of my room. I crept over to the front desk to grab the master key while Lupe tiptoed out the back. With the master key, we opened up one of the empty guest rooms and went inside. I giggled, flipping on the TV to one of the music channels José had added for us. "Ain't No Mountain High Enough" by Marvin Gaye and Tammi Terrell was playing. I turned the volume way up and jumped onto the bed.

"Ain't no mountain high enough!" I sang, using the remote control as my mic.

Lupe ran into the bathroom, returned with the hair dryer, which she used as her mic, and jumped onto the other bed.

"Ain't no valley low enough!" she sang into the hair dryer.

"Ain't no river wide enough," we sang together. "To keep me from getting to you!"

That night, we sang our hearts out, jumping on top of the beds. Lupe smiled and wiped her eyes as she sang. It was the most fun we'd both had in months.

CHAPTER 42

After the meeting with Ms. Patel, we doubled down on Operation Save José, turning the front desk into an assembly line. Hank and Fred looked up the addresses of politicians, while Lupe and I wrote letters, Mrs. Q and Mrs. T stuffed envelopes, and Billy Bob licked stamps.

At school on Friday, Lupe continued writing letters during recess while I sat in my special lesson with Mrs. Welch. The recess tutorials were going well, especially now that we'd moved on from grammar to figurative language. Today, Mrs. Welch was going over personification and metaphors.

"I liked this one you wrote," Mrs. Welch said, picking up my latest essay from her desk. *"My parents may be on side streets now, but one day, they'll be on the main road."*

"It's just something they say in Chinese." I blushed, slightly embarrassed I had written that down.

"Well, it's a good metaphor," Mrs. Welch said. "And I liked this: *Some of the immigrants who come to the motel on Wednesdays, they have it even harder than us. Some of them haven't yet found the side streets. They are just forging their way through thick brush, with only the stars to guide them,*" Mrs. Welch read. She reached up to touch her cheek. Was she *crying*?

As she handed me back my paper, I looked up to see the grade, expecting another C. But this time, it was an A–.

"The minus is for some minor grammatical mistakes," she said. "Otherwise it would have been an A."

An A– from Mrs. Welch! Wow! That was like an A++ from a normal teacher! A smile stretched across my face as I clutched my paper proudly. Lupe was thrilled for me and we ran all the way home, our arms swinging wildly, excited to get back to Operation Save José!

. . .

By noon on Saturday, stacks of letters lay on the front desk, ready to go out. There was a pile for congressmen, congresswomen, and US senators; a pile for the state assembly and state senate; and a third pile to mayors and county supervisors.

Dear Senator,

José Garcia, age 38, is currently being held in San Diego County Jail awaiting deportation proceedings. Please do not let Immigration deport Mr. Garcia. He is a husband, father, skilled and hardworking Californian. He has an 11-year-old daughter. Deporting him will separate him from his family. He has good moral character and no criminal record. He has been in this country for more than eight years and has worked in the fields in the Central Valley picking grapes, as a pizza deliveryman, and as a cable repairman in a motel in Anaheim, California. Mr. Garcia is an

honest and hardworking immigrant who has contributed greatly to the California economy.

We urge you, kind senator, from the bottom
of our hearts, to please grant José Garcia an
adjustment of status so that he can be reunited
with his family. His trial is in four weeks. Please
contact us at the number below if you have any
questions. Thank you.

Sincerely,
Californians Against José Garcia Deportation

It was Hank's idea to call ourselves the "Californians Against
José Garcia Deportation." He said the letters would sound more
powerful if they came from a group. And what a group we were.
Hank even ordered us T-shirts, with artwork designed by Lupe!

Meanwhile, immigrants continued swinging by the Calivista,
attracted to our sign. To each customer who came in, we gave a copy
of the flyer of Lupe's mom. The petition Lupe and I created was
getting longer and longer, thanks in part to all the help from our
Kids for Kids members. We made an extra petition just for the motel
customers. To our great delight, our customers all signed their
names. My dad happily offered discounts for the night, but to his
surprise, some of them didn't want discounts. They insisted on paying full price for the rooms!

The immigrants came from all over, from Mexico and the
Dominican Republic to as far away as the Philippines and Kenya!
Hank was tickled pink to see immigrants who looked like him.

"My people!" he warmly welcomed them.

On Sunday, the cash register was filled again. "Hey, look!" I said, showing my parents and Hank the stacks of cash. We called up all the paper investors, including Mr. Cooper. He was busy on a conference call but said he'd look at the numbers and call us back later.

A few of the kids from Kids for Kids came to join the Operation Save José effort, including Jason, who stopped by after his cooking class. When Lupe saw Jason, she moved her body across the front desk to try to cover up the flyers of her mom.

"What's he doing here?" she whispered to me.

"I heard that," Jason said, picking up an envelope. He reached for a letter to stuff into the envelope but accidentally reached for the wrong pile and picked up a flyer.

"No!" Lupe said, yanking it away.

I looked at the two of them, puzzled.

"We have to talk," Lupe said, and took me by the arm, pulling me to our room and closing the door behind her. "I don't want Jason over here, looking at that stuff about my mom. He and Mrs. Yao threw me and my mom out of their house when I was eight!"

I listened in stunned silence as Lupe told me what had happened three years before. Her mother used to clean Mr. Yao's house. While she cleaned, Jason and Lupe would hang out in his room. They were good friends then.

"One day, Mrs. Yao came home and found the two of us rolling around on the floor. We were just arm wrestling, but she grabbed me and pulled me into her study. She said she was disgusted with me," Lupe said. "And she fired me and my mom."

I put my hands to my mouth.

"I thought Jason would stand up for me, but he didn't do anything! He didn't even come out of his room!" Lupe sat down on the bed and pointed at the door. "He says he wants to help, but where was he then?"

I gazed at the door. I could feel her anger melting a hole in the wood and knew exactly how she felt. It was how I felt when Mrs. Yao pulled Jason out of the motel room that day. "I'm so sorry, Lupe."

She looked up from my cherry blossom bedspread. "Please, can you just ask him to leave?" she said.

I nodded. "Of course." I left her in the room and asked, as gently as I could, that Jason go.

He looked back at me, eyes welling with hurt. "What'd I do?"

I shook my head, not knowing quite how to tell him. "You just have to go," I said again.

Jason stomped out of the front office. As he threw open the door, he shouted, "You'll be sorry, Mia Tang! I have feelings too!"

I put my head down on the front desk, feeling a little bad for kicking Jason out. But as I peeked over at my best friend, standing by the door of my bedroom, I hoped she knew I would always have her back.

CHAPTER 43

"Folks, if you're joining us now, you're looking at live footage from City Hall, where some seventy to a hundred thousand demonstrators have gathered to protest Governor Pete Wilson and Proposition 187," the newscaster reported.

It was the last Sunday of October, the day of the big march, and Lupe and I were taking a break from stuffing envelopes. We leaned in toward the TV as the reporter pulled one of the marchers aside, a white man, and asked him why he was protesting.

The guy, in sunglasses and a fedora hat, said to the camera, "I'm here because this proposition is not against illegals, it's against children!"

"Lupe," I said, an idea popping into my head as I spoke, "we should go to the march! Think how many signatures we could get on our petition!"

"Are you sure—" she started to say, but I'd already jumped up.

"Hank!" I called.

Hank came into the manager's quarters and looked at the TV, his eyes transfixed. A guy from the Southern Christian Leadership Conference was shouting at the podium, "California will not stand on a platform of bigotry, racism, and scapegoating!"

"Wow! We should go see this!" Hank said.

"That's what I was thinking!" I said, reaching for the petition. It was ten pages long now, with all the signatures from the customers and from the kids in our club, some of whom had taken it to church for people to sign. "We could take our petition!"

Lupe still looked uneasy. "But what if there are cops there?" she asked.

I thought about what Jason said about how there might be all sorts of crazy racist people there. But it didn't look that way on TV.

Hank reassured Lupe, "We don't have to protest. And we can leave anytime. But it'd be great for you to see it with your own eyes."

"Why?" Lupe asked.

"Because it's not right, what's happening. And all those people marching—" Hank pointed at the TV. "They think it's not right. And I want you to see that. I want you to feel that. Right here." He put his hand to his chest.

"Please, Lupe," I said. "Can we go?"

Her feet remained glued to the frayed brown carpet, though. "I wish I could ask my mom. . . ."

Hank walked over to the front desk and grabbed the blue Yankees hat that we used all last year to signal to immigrants when Mr. Yao wasn't around and they could come in.

"You can wear a hat," he said, putting it on Lupe's head. "How's that? No one will recognize you out there."

Lupe reached up and felt the power of the blue hat with both hands, a hat that had protected so many immigrants before her. Finally, she nodded.

"YES!" Hank and I shouted, high-fiving each other.

We ran out the back and jumped into Hank's car. Hank put his foot to the gas while I rolled down the window and told my mom where we were going. As Hank sped down the 5 Freeway, Lupe pulled her blue hat down tightly on her head.

"Here we go!" Hank shouted.

. . .

We could hear the march even before we saw it. There was a pounding on the ground, almost like a roar, as great masses of people surged down the streets of downtown Los Angeles. Overhead, a helicopter circled. The traffic forced Hank's car to a stop and Lupe pointed out the window at the marchers. "Look!" she cried.

The protestors were crossing a highway bridge. There were hundreds and hundreds of them, men and women, white, black, Latino, Asian, and Native American, mothers and fathers carrying children on their necks and backs. Many were waving the American flag and the California flag. A few were even waving the Mexican flag. Lupe put her knuckles in her mouth, overwhelmed with emotion. The marchers carried signs that said *Stop Prop 187!*; *Fences are for pigs, not people!*; *Immigrants are People Too!*; and *No such thing as an illegal alien!* I pointed to a sign that read *We didn't cross the border, the border crossed us!*

Hank handed us little packets of tissues. I hadn't even realized I was crying. Hot tears glistened on Lupe's face too. It was just so overwhelming to see.

As we dried our eyes, Hank found parking. We got out and walked over to City Hall, where there was a stage set up with a mic.

"We are workers, not criminals!" a Latina woman shouted into the mic.

"Sí, asi se dice!" Lupe shouted, cheering and handing out the petition to all those around her.

As the signatures filled the page, an Asian man took the stage. "This proposition is an insult to all immigrants!" he said.

I clapped until my hands hurt. I wished my dad could have been there to see it.

"If it passes, we are all suspect!" a black man from Jamaica added. The crowd erupted in applause, and I felt his words, right in my heart. Hank was right, you had to be there.

Lupe and I worked quickly, gathering signatures as people spoke onstage. When a thirty-seven-year-old factory worker took the mic and said he was an undocumented immigrant, Lupe looked up.

A little boy joined him onstage. "This is my little boy!" the man told the audience. I looked over at Lupe. Her chin was trembling. "He's six years old. He didn't do anything wrong! You want to take away his education? You want to take him out of the first grade?"

"NO!" the crowd shouted.

With that, the crowd started chanting, "No 187! No Re-Pete!" With each thunderous "No," I looked out at the sea of faces, every single one of them carrying hopes and dreams and fears, just like Lupe's family and mine. As the crowd cheered wildly, Lupe took off the blue Yankees hat and threw it high in the air.

CHAPTER 44

At school, everyone was talking about the big march. Mrs. Welch went and got a copy of the newspaper and laid it out on a big table. We all leaned over and looked.

I peered down, expecting to see headlines that read, "Tens of Thousands Take to the Streets to Renounce Hatred and Racism." Instead, the headlines said, "Sea of Brown Faces Marching Through Los Angeles Antagonizes Voters."

"What's *antagonize* mean?" I asked Mrs. Welch.

"It means you do something that makes people not like you," she said, frowning at the article.

"Really? But we were there —" I said, looking over at Lupe.

"We were there too!" Kareña said excitedly.

"That's amazing that you guys all went!" Mrs. Welch said. "What was it like? Can you describe it for us?"

"It was . . ." I paused for the right adjective.

"Electrifying," Lupe answered.

At that afternoon's club meeting, we were all still talking about the march, except Jason. He was sulking.

He finally came up to me after the meeting. "You hurt my feelings, Mia Tang," he said as we walked back to class. "I don't understand why you kicked me out the other day!"

"It's complicated, Jason," I tried to explain, then stopped when I saw the wall by the bathroom. In small, dry-erase marker were the words *Go back to your own school! This one is ours!*

I stared at *This one is ours*, feeling the anger pulsate on my lips.

"C'mon, let's go," Jason said, trying to pull me away.

"No," I said. I went up to the wall and tried to rub the words out with my fingers, but they wouldn't come off. Still, I rubbed and rubbed. Jason finally went and got me some water, and we worked together, rubbing until the white plaster of the wall shone through.

. . .

Who wrote that on the wall?

The thought looped in my head all afternoon. I didn't tell Lupe about it. She'd been through enough lately.

Hank was inside the manager's quarters watching the news when we got back. Reports of hate crimes were on the rise after the march, the newscaster said. A woman in Pasadena tried to cash her paycheck, but the bank teller refused to serve her unless she showed her green card. A man's house burned down in a fire, and when he called up the insurance company, the representative told him to "go back to his country." All over the state of California, immigrants were called horrible names and turned away from stores, banks, restaurants, and even theme parks.

The phone in the front office rang.

"Calivista Motel, how can I help you?" I answered.

"Hi, this is Karen from Senator Feinstein's office. Is this the Garcia residence?"

Did she just say *Senator*?

"Just a minute!" I said, gesturing wildly to get Lupe's attention. "It's Senator Feinstein's office!" I whispered loudly.

Lupe ran over and picked up the phone while Hank and I went into my room to listen in on the extension.

"Are you Mr. Garcia's daughter?" the woman asked.

"Yes!" Lupe said.

"We've received your letter about your dad. Senator Feinstein would like to say that she will be throwing her support against the deportation of your father, José Garcia."

"I'm sorry, can you repeat that? Did you say *against*, or *for*?" Lupe asked.

"Against," the woman repeated. "We'll try our best to help get your dad out. And Lupe?"

"Yes?" Lupe's voice was a tiny squeak.

"Senator Feinstein is so sorry you're going through this. We all are."

"Thank you."

The woman hung up the phone, and Hank and I whooped for joy as we ran out to congratulate Lupe.

"AHHHHHH!!!" she screamed. She took my hand and we jumped up and down.

"Senator FEINSTEIN — that's big! We gotta tell the media!" Hank yelled, plunging into publicist mode. As Hank started making a list of places we could contact, Lupe and I called over the rest of the weeklies and my parents.

"Definitely the Latino media," my dad suggested.

"That's a great idea!" Billy Bob said. "And the local TV channels — Channel 7 and KNBC?"

"Don't forget radio," Fred said.

Hank grabbed a pen and a notepad and wrote all this down. "I'll get right on it," he said.

I drummed my fingers, quietly mulling. I had an idea that was going to be a long shot, but it was worth a try.

Lupe turned to Hank. "You really think they'll want to report on this? With everything that's going on?" she asked, glancing hesitantly over at the TV.

"I think so," Hank said. "You saw how many people were at that march. There are folks out there who care."

"Folks like us," I added. I hopped off the stool and placed my hand on top of Lupe's. Hank leaned over and placed his dark brown hand on top of mine, and my parents added their hands on top of Hank's. And one by one, the weeklies added their hands too, until it was one big mountain of hands.

I looked around at all the love and hope and compassion in the room.

The tide was turning, I could feel it.

CHAPTER 45

That night, I worked on my secret idea—a letter to the editor.

Dear Editor,

As an immigrant child, I am deeply saddened by all the Prop 187 and anti-immigrant sentiments in the news. They are not reflective of the community of people I know and love. America is a country built by immigrants. People from all over the world come here to settle, like my parents, who gave up their careers as an engineer and a scientist so that I might have a brighter future, and my best friend's dad, José Garcia, who is one of the kindest, most giving people I know and who has taught me many things, including the value of hard work.

José Garcia came over from Mexico eight years ago. For years, he toiled in the Central Valley heat, picking grapes off the prickly vines until his fingers bled. Some days, the sulfur and chemicals were so bad, he coughed himself to sleep. Later, he became a pizza deliveryman, risking his life to deliver pizzas! Then after that, he taught himself how to fix the cable and became a highly skilled cable repairman. You won't believe the channels he can add to your TV!

He has a wife and a daughter, who is 11 years old, like me. His daughter's math is so good, she's going to become one of those crazy math people like my mom, who has pieces of math in her pockets.

But her dad may not be there to see it because as we speak, he is in San Diego County Jail facing deportation proceedings. I urge you, kind editors and readers, to write to your congressmen and your senators to STOP the deportation of José Garcia. And to vote NO on Prop 187. It is inhumane to take education away from children. We have done nothing wrong. We are the future, and we have hopes and dreams, just like you.

Vote NO to hate, NO to deporting José Garcia, NO on Proposition 187, and NO to Governor Wilson.

Sincerely,

Mia Tang

Age 11

I reread my letter a thousand times, proofreading it according to all the grammar rules Mrs. Welch taught me. She was right, learning the rules made me sure, not just guessing. As I was finishing up the letter, Lupe came bouncing into my room.

"Guess what?" she asked. "I just got off the phone with a reporter for a Latino newspaper. She wants to interview me!"

"She's not the only one," Hank said, walking in behind her, his eyes shining. "I just got off the phone with Channel 2. They want you on camera."

"Channel 2? As in *TV*?" Lupe asked.

"That's GREAT!" I said.

But Lupe took a step backward. "I don't think that's such a good idea. . . ."

"Listen to me, it's going to be fine," Hank reassured her. "I'll be right there with you. It'll be tomorrow after school."

But Lupe's hands shook the way my dad's did whenever the health department came by to inspect.

In class the next day, Lupe sat at her desk looking a bit green and nauseous while the other kids talked about Michael Huffington, a politician running for Senate. The papers reported that he and his wife had employed an undocumented immigrant to take care of their kids — for five years.

"Five years?" Stuart shrieked, squeezing his face with his hands like the kid in *Home Alone*.

Bethany Brett was playing with her ruby necklace. "My dad says everyone needs illegal aliens to clean their house and take care of the kids."

Lupe muttered to Bethany, "They can do a whole lot more than that."

"What did you say?" Bethany asked.

"I said, they can do a lot more than that," Lupe repeated, louder this time.

I looked up in surprise. *All right, Lupe!*

"And it's not *illegal aliens*," Lupe added. "It's *undocumented immigrants*."

Bethany Brett rolled her eyes. "Whatever."

Then Mrs. Welch said, "Did you guys know that Michael J. Fox and Arnold Schwarzenegger worked illegally in the US?"

"Schwarzenegger?" Stuart asked.

With that, my classmates instantly dropped immigration and launched into a debate on which was better, *The Terminator* or *Terminator 2*. I just smiled at Lupe and Mrs. Welch. They'd both surprised me so much that day. Their comments made me feel like this was *my* school, no matter what anyone scribbled on the walls.

. . .

I found Jason sitting on the floor in the hall later that day, right below the spot where we'd rubbed off the awful graffiti.

"Hey," he said.

"Anything?" I asked, pointing to the wall.

He scooted over so I could see. No new words. Thank goodness.

"So you gonna tell me why you kicked me out the other day?" he asked. "I thought we were friends. . . ."

"We *are* friends." I sighed and sat down next to him. I had about ten minutes before Mrs. Welch sent someone to look for me in the bathroom. "If you really want to know, it has to do with what went down when Lupe and her mom worked for you guys. You kind of kicked her out first?"

He started shaking his head—but suddenly he gasped, his face turning a mortified red.

"That was ages ago," he said. "I was only like eight years old!"

I took a deep breath, not knowing how to explain to him that even if it seemed like a long time ago in his mind, to Lupe, the memory was still very much alive. The wound had solidified, growing more powerful and pungent, like my dad's leftover oil.

"Anyway," he went on, "my *mom's* the one who did that, not me. She's the one who got all mad!"

I turned to him. "Like she got mad at me at the motel that day?" I asked.

There was a flash of guilt in Jason's eyes. Then he looked down.

"I'm sorry for that," he muttered. He looked genuinely embarrassed, and I could tell he hadn't forgotten about it either.

"It's okay," I muttered back. I leaned over and bumped my shoulder with his. "See, that wasn't so bad."

Jason shook his head. "But I can't apologize to Lupe *now*. It'd be so weird."

I looked into Jason's eyes and said, "It's never too late to say sorry." I started getting up, but he reached out and touched my arm.

"Mia, you gotta understand, I was little. And I was scared."

I thought about this for a second.

"It's okay to be scared," I finally told him. "But you know what's even scarier? Realizing something is wrong and not saying anything."

Jason glanced at me as I reached to pull him up.

"You can do it," I said. "You've done it before."

CHAPTER 46

I didn't tell Lupe about what Jason said by the bathroom. She was already on edge walking home from school. I could almost hear her nerves rattling around in her stomach as she went over what she was going to say to the TV reporter in a few hours.

We got back to find the living room in the manager's quarters completely transformed. Not only was it dusted and vacuumed, my parents' bed was gone, making the living room look more like a living room. I smiled, remembering what Lupe once said about how the definition of success in this country was if you had a living room without a bed in it. Well, we finally got there, even if it was only for an hour!

Mrs. Q went and got some flowers. At 5:30, when the reporter was supposed to arrive, Lupe started freaking out.

"I can't do this," she said, shaking her head and jiggling her legs. "I'll do the newspaper interview, but I can't go on TV!"

We all gathered around, but Lupe wedged her chin between her knees and covered her face with her hands. Hank sat next to her on the couch and promised he wasn't going to let the network use her real name or show her face—he had arranged it so that they would blur it out.

"But what if they forget?" Lupe said into her knees. "I could get deported!"

"I'm going to make sure they don't forget," Hank insisted. "That's what I'm here for. I'm the Marketing Director, remember? You have nothing to worry about."

Lupe looked up at him. "That's easy for you to say! You have papers!"

I squeezed in beside Hank. "Hey, remember that card you wrote?" I said. *"You can't win if you don't play?"*

Lupe nodded.

I went to get it from my room. I found it next to my nightstand, the little card that had helped me so many times last year. Its edges were all worn, and the paper had yellowed, but it still had life to it. Gently, I placed it back in Lupe's hand.

"Now's the time to play!" I said. "We have to hit them with everything we've got!"

"But what if . . . what if . . ." Lupe's lips trembled.

Hank knelt down besides Lupe. "Remember how I got rejected for the line of credit? Thirty-one bank managers looked into my eyes and said, 'We don't like you, and we don't trust you.' " Hank shook his head. "When I got to the last one, I was scared. I thought about giving up. And I'm not saying my fear was anything like your fear right now, because it's not."

Lupe unwedged her chin, listening closely.

"But I have fear too," Hank went on. "I have fear just driving down the street, that's why I put a sticker on my car. I'm afraid of being pulled over. I have fear walking into a grocery store, maybe they're gonna accuse me of stealing something. I have fear just putting on a *pair of sweatpants*!" He pointed to his khaki dress slacks.

I was wondering why he chose to wear them every day, even when it was 102 degrees outside and every single other person was in shorts.

"I have fear every day," Hank told Lupe. "But let me tell you something about fear: If you don't control it, it controls you."

Lupe gazed down at the worn-out card. Then she pressed it tightly between her palms.

"You ready to not let it control you?" Hank asked.

Lupe's eyes slid over to the hook on the wall where her father's work jacket hung.

"I'm going to be right there," Hank said. "I'm going to make sure nothing happens to you. Do you trust me?"

Lupe nodded, slowly.

"I trust you."

CHAPTER 47

Lupe's interview aired the next day—on Halloween. We all crowded around the living room and watched the footage instead of going trick-or-treating. Lupe's face was blurred out. You could only see her neck and her shirt. She was sitting in the manager's quarters, wearing her *NO ON PROP 187* shirt that we got at the march.

"I just want my dad to stay here so we can be a family," Lupe said in the interview. "My dad's a good person. He's never been in trouble before. He works so hard."

Her voice was bold and strong. It was like she'd bundled up all her worries and hid them behind cabinets and beds, the way my mom did with loose electrical cords.

She went on to describe how her dad got up at the crack of dawn each day, climbed onto the roofs of houses and buildings under the hot sun, and never took a single day off—not even on Christmas, when someone (Mr. Yao, I happened to know) demanded José come over to fix the cable so his son (that would be Jason) could watch movies in his room.

As the camera cut to pictures of her dad, I put my arm around Lupe. I was so proud of her. The last few weeks had been really hard, and I knew she was scared of going on TV. But tonight, she had enough courage to power a city.

The reporter asked Lupe what she thought of Prop 187. "Do you think it had anything to do with your dad getting picked up?"

"I think Prop 187 makes it okay to target immigrants," Lupe replied. "And I don't think that's fair. We're good people. We're not here to make trouble. We want to work hard and succeed, just like everyone else."

"Woo-hoo!" Hank cheered, jumping up and clapping. "Well said!"

The weeklies and my parents all hugged Lupe when the interview was over and congratulated her on what an amazing, awe-inspiring job she did!

"Girl, you nailed it," I said, beaming at my best friend. Lupe grinned and gave me a high five.

Just then, the phone rang.

"Lupe!" my mom exclaimed. "It's your mother!"

CHAPTER 48

When Lupe heard her mom's voice on the phone, she started sobbing.

"Mami!" she cried. "I thought you were dead!"

As the two of them exchanged words in Spanish, my mom gripped my hand. I tried to make out what they were saying, but my Spanish was limited to the most basic check-in and check-out terms.

"No, Mami, stay there," Lupe said in English.

I'd been hoping that Mrs. Garcia had made it back to the States and was just lost, wandering around somewhere in San Diego, but as Lupe hung up and then sat there, staring at the phone in her hands, I realized she must still be in Mexico.

"She tried to cross over but the coyotes she hired were bad," Lupe explained. "They took all her money but wouldn't help her cross. . . ." Her voice trailed off.

"That's terrible!" I said.

"She couldn't call us because she didn't have any money," Lupe said. "And when she saw our flyer—"

"Wait a minute, she saw our flyer??" I asked.

Lupe nodded. "A woman at a bus station had one. That's how my mom was finally able to call us—the woman let her use her phone."

I couldn't believe that our little flyer somehow made it all the way down to Mexico and helped Mrs. Garcia get back in touch with us.

"I'm so relieved she's okay," Lupe said, wiping a tear from her cheek. "I really thought she was dead. . . ."

My mother scooped Lupe up into her arms and declared, "This calls for a celebration!" She turned to my dad and suggested we lock the front office and all go out for a Halloween dinner. Lupe and the weeklies and I immediately seconded this idea — it was even better than trick-or-treating.

My dad said, "You guys go ahead. I'll stay behind and watch the motel."

"Oh, c'mon," I protested. "We never get to go out all together."

"But there's so much to do," he said, looking wearily toward the laundry room. I knew what he was thinking. It was the same thing he thought every night — that the towels needed to be washed, the sodas needed to be refilled in the vending machine. The recycling needed to be sorted. The pool leaves needed to be gathered. The list was as long as my arm.

"Just this once," my mom said. "The towels will still be there tomorrow."

My dad hesitated. "But it'll be more expensive if we all go. . . ."

Hank put a hand on my dad's back. "Once in a while, you gotta live a little, buddy. Otherwise, you'll burn out."

My dad shook his head. "I don't believe in burnout. That's an American thing."

I wanted to roll my eyes. Instead, I tried to put it to him another way.

"What about celebrating with family?" I asked my dad. "Isn't that a Chinese thing?"

Lupe and I looked up at him with big, hopeful smiles on our faces, and my dad relented.

"All right," he said finally. "Let's do it."

As we piled into the car, my mother smiled at my dad, practically giddy with excitement, and he laughed. It was a wonderful sight, seeing my parents both so happy, and I reached out with my hands, pretend clicked, and called out, "Eggplant!"

This time, my mom held up two fingers and smiled at the camera.

CHAPTER 49

We took three cars to Country Family Café, a local diner a few blocks away. There were so many of us, the waitress had to move some tables together so we could all fit. After we ordered burgers, salads, and sweet potato fries for the table, Hank raised his glass of lemonade high up in the air.

"To Lupe on TV!" he said, and we all cheered.

She smiled. "No matter what happens, I'll always remember what you guys have done for me."

"Whoa, whoa, whoa." I shook my head at her. "What's this *no matter what happens* talk? There is only one *what* that's going to happen, and that's getting your dad out of jail and your mom back from Mexico!"

"You really think so?" Lupe asked.

"I know so!" I said. "You were fantastic!" I pointed to her and announced to the whole restaurant, "Future broadcast journalist right here, everybody!"

Lupe's cheeks flushed as several heads turned. "I wish my parents had seen it," she said.

"We'll get a copy from the network," Hank said. "José can watch it when he gets out. He'll be so proud."

Our food came and I was just reaching for a fry when my best friend's voice filled the room. We looked up and saw Lupe's interview was airing *again* on the big TV in the diner! We erupted in cheers.

"Wooo!!!" we shouted. "That's our girl!"

Two white construction workers in the booth next to us looked from the TV to Lupe. "Is that you?" they asked.

Lupe froze.

Everything got really quiet. My hands balled into fists and my stomach tightened as one of the guys got up and walked over to our table. Hank got out of the booth and stood up tall.

"She's with me," he said, staring the guy down.

My mom reached for my dad's hand, and I held on to Lupe's.

But the guy simply turned to Lupe and said, "I just want to say, I'm sorry you're going through this."

It took us a second to realize that was it. That's all the man wanted to say. As Hank sat back down, Lupe thanked the man and offered him one of our sweet potato fries.

. . .

Later that night, in our room, Lupe asked me if I could hear her heart hammering when the guy walked over to our table. I couldn't; I was too busy listening to my own. It felt so weird to go from total terror to surprise kindness, kind of like one of those roller coasters where you think you're going forward only to lunge backward. At the thought of roller coasters, I smiled. I wondered if we could finally go to Disneyland to ride Space Mountain after the trial. If we won. *When* we won. I turned my head on the pillow to face Lupe.

"Hey, I've been wanting to tell you, but with everything going on . . ." I took a breath. "Jason feels really bad about what happened."

She didn't say anything.

"You think you could ever forgive him?" I waited for her reply and gazed out the window, watching the clouds float across the glowing, full moon.

"Well, he hasn't exactly apologized," Lupe finally said.

"Maybe he'll surprise you."

"Maybe."

I smiled at the moon, thinking about how nice that would be. Then maybe Jason and Lupe and I could go to Disneyland together!

"Good night," Lupe said, yawning.

"Good night," I whispered back.

"You know what tomorrow is, right?" she asked. "Tomorrow is November."

I nodded in the darkness. In less than one week, Californians would vote to decide Lupe's future. I hoped that when they went into the voting booths, they'd pleasantly surprise us, just like the kind man did at dinner tonight.

CHAPTER 50

Jason walked up to me and Lupe at school the next day.

"You were so great on TV last night!" he said to her.

Lupe and I glanced at each other. "How'd you know it was her?" I asked. "The face was blurred out."

"Please, I could recognize that living room anywhere," he said. "I've been there a million times, remember?"

Oh, yeah.

Jason turned back to Lupe. His voice quieted as he looked down at his hands. "There's something I need to say. . . . I'm sorry about the way I treated you, back when we were little. It was wrong."

Lupe lifted her eyes slowly.

"I should have stood up for you," Jason said.

"Why didn't you?"

"I . . ." Jason swallowed. "I was too scared." He glanced at me. "But as someone recently told me, what's even scarier is not saying anything about it. I hope I'm not too late."

I marveled at him. He really had changed bucketloads.

"Will you be my friend again?"

Lupe nodded. As they shook hands, I put my arms around them both and looked on with pride.

• • •

Later that day, Jason came over and helped me stuff letters to more congresswomen and congressmen while Hank took Lupe down to San Diego again to visit her dad. As he worked, Jason told me his family was going to move next week into a smaller house.

"But you'll still go to the same school, right?" I asked.

"Yeah," he said, licking an envelope.

"That's good. Have you seen the new house?" I asked. "What's it like?"

Jason shrugged. "It's okay," he said simply. Without saying anything more, he reached over to turn on the radio in the living room. The voice of the radio show host filled the air.

"And did you guys hear the interview last night of the little girl whose dad's about to be deported?" the host asked.

Jason and I both looked up. "Lupe's on the radio!" I shrieked. Jason got so excited, he threw all the stamps in his hand up in the air. It was a confetti of stamps!

"His name is José Garcia," the host went on, "and he's a cable repairman with no criminal record. His daughter says he's never taken a single day off, not even on *Christmas*. Can you imagine that?"

Jason shouted at the radio, "Hey! For your information, *Honey, I Shrunk the Kids* was on!"

Yeah, and it became *Honey, I Have to Work on Christmas.*

"And now the poor guy's facing deportation. If he gets deported, he may never see his daughter again. His daughter, by the way, what an incredible girl. Straight-A student, super articulate," the radio host said. "I was so impressed with her. I'll tell ya, I couldn't do that when I was her age, stand there so poised and speak so eloquently on TV."

Jason and I grinned at each other. "Go, Lupe!" we cheered.

The cohost spoke then. "It just goes to show, if Prop 187 passes, that's the kind of kid we're going to be kicking out of our schools. Is that what California really wants?"

"NO!!" I shouted to the radio.

"Let's hear from the listeners," the first guy suggested. Their telephone rang with a call.

"Hi. This is Tim Webster calling from Northridge. I don't care that she's a straight-A student, she's still an illegal, and I say, get rid of 'em. Illegal immigrants mooch off the US government. They come here, have babies, steal jobs —"

I reached over and turned off the radio. Everything was quiet for a long minute. I looked down at the stack of envelopes in my lap. Jason touched my arm.

"Hey, don't be sad. I used to think that too," he reminded me. "And now I don't."

I thought back to our first conversation about Prop 187 in Jason's room, when he threw the paper airplane at me. It was hard to believe that was just a few months ago.

"Too bad you can't vote," I said.

"I can when I'm eighteen," Jason declared proudly.

I envied his certainty. Even though we had green cards, my parents and I weren't citizens yet. Was I going to be able to vote when I turned eighteen? I hoped so.

The phone at the front desk rang, and when I picked it up, Mrs. Q shouted, "Turn to Channel 2!"

I pointed to the TV, and Jason went over and turned it on. Channel 2 was showing live footage from right outside San Diego

County Jail. A dozen people were chanting, "Free José Garcia! Free José Garcia!" Men and women and kids of all different colors and ethnicities were holding large signs for Lupe's dad!

Jason put his head up close to the screen and pointed to the small figure to the right.

"Look! There's Lupe!" he cried. I ran over and knelt beside him in front of the screen. He was right — I recognized Lupe's long wavy hair and her clothes! We waved to her, even though she couldn't see us.

As the sun gleamed above the barbed wire fence, Lupe smiled at the people who had turned out for her dad.

I wished she could see the look on her face. She'd want to draw it over and over and over again.

CHAPTER 51

The night traffic had receded to a dull murmur by the time Lupe and Hank came home. But before I could tell Lupe about them being on TV, the shrill ring of the telephone disrupted me. I picked it up.

"I saw the latest numbers," Mr. Cooper said instead of hello. "The occupancy rates are up, which is good."

"Yup! Thanks to all the immigrants, we've had a lot more people checking in," I told him. I bit my tongue from adding, *Told ya the sign was good!*

"But the total profits are still low."

"True," I admitted. "That's because we gave some people a discount. If only we had more rooms to put people. . . ." I reached out and ran my fingers over the keys hanging under the front desk.

"Well," Mr. Cooper said. "I called because I'm going to hold on to my shares. For now. But I want to see these profits back up soon."

He didn't say when or what he was going to do if that didn't happen. Still, we all slept soundly that night for the first time in weeks.

The next morning, I woke up to urgent banging on the front office window. Mrs. T was carrying a copy of the *Los Angeles Times*.

"Mia! Wake up! You're in the paper!"

CHAPTER 52

Mrs. T set a copy of the newspaper on my bed and turned to the inside of the front section. There, published in the Letters to the Editor section, was my letter!

I couldn't believe my eyes! I took the paper from Mrs. T and ran through the manager's quarters screaming, "I'm an author!!! I'm an author!!!"

Lupe leaped out of her rollaway bed, and my parents came over to see what all the commotion was about. When they saw my name in the paper, my dad took me in his arms and spun me around.

"My lucky penny!" He kissed my hair. "You did it!"

"This is so amazing!" Lupe said. Her eyes danced across the page as she read my words. They printed my letter word for word, and even added a little cartoon of an immigrant kid watching the Prop 187 ads on TV.

"Oh, Mia, I'm so proud of you!" my mom said.

I grinned from ear to ear as I soaked up their words. My parents called to Hank, and when he saw my letter, he lifted me off my feet.

"Hot diggity dog! Our Mia's a real writer now!" He beamed. "I knew you could do it!"

It was the most amazing feeling in the world, seeing my words in print. As I walked to school that morning carrying the newspaper in my hand, I felt the entire world open up, my lungs filling with possibility!

. . .

At school, the classroom was buzzing with chatter. The election was next week, and everyone was guessing who would win. I waited until my classmates settled down and we all got back in our seats before raising my hand.

"Yes, Mia?" Mrs. Welch called with a nod. "Do you have something to share with the class?"

Gently, I unfolded the newspaper on my desk. The other kids peered curiously at it, as though maybe there was a pet iguana hidden inside. But there was something even better.

"I . . ." I looked down at the paper, the words too magical to say.

"Mia was published in today's newspaper," Lupe announced.

"Really??" Mrs. Welch's eyes sparkled. She gestured for the paper and put on her reading glasses. "Let's see it!"

As she read my letter out loud, I sat at my desk nervously, wondering what the other kids were going to say and what errors Mrs. Welch was going to find. A misplaced comma or word that ought to be capitalized? There had to be something.

But all I got when she finished reading was the smile of a proud teacher. "Marvelous," she said. "Just marvelous."

For the rest of the day, I felt as light as air. At lunch, the kids in our club read my letter out loud. They were SO proud of me. I bounced on the balls of my feet as we celebrated our win—and that's exactly what it felt like. Like *we* were published. We were heard.

Before the end of the school day, Mrs. Welch asked if she could borrow the newspaper to make a copy to hang on the school wall. As I handed her the newspaper, I thought, *wow, if I can get someone like Mrs. Welch to change her mind with my words, then maybe, just maybe, Californians will do the right thing.*

CHAPTER 53

My dad came to pick me up after school. He was taking me out to our favorite spot by the lake to celebrate.

"I'm so proud of you," he said as we sat down on our favorite patch of grass, underneath the big cypress tree.

"For getting published in the newspaper?" I asked. I smiled, thinking back to last year when he gave me the sparkly green pencil, which I still had, and encouraged me to write everything down.

"Not just that. For helping your friend Lupe and not giving in to Mr. Cooper about the sign. It shows you have *yi qi*."

The crimson autumn leaves swayed gently above us.

"What's *yi qi*?" I asked.

"*Yi qi* means loyalty," he said. "It means sticking up for your friends. It's one of the most important Chinese values."

"You have it too," I pointed out, thinking about how he always went to bat for his immigrant friends. If I had a few drops of *yi qi*, my dad had an ocean of it.

My dad chuckled. "That's right, I do." He reached over and patted my head. "You may be becoming more American. But you're still very Chinese inside."

I leaned my head against my father's arm and snuggled up to

him under the warm sun. I hadn't realized I'd been waiting to hear those words until right then.

"Thanks, Dad." I smiled.

Maybe being Chinese wasn't about liking red bean shaved ice or having serious chopsticks skills, I thought as I looked out onto the peaceful lake. Maybe it had to do with *yi qi* and all sorts of other Chinese values living inside me, just waiting to be discovered.

. . .

My mother was waiting at the front desk when we got home. She was taking me and Lupe shopping to celebrate my being published in the newspaper and Lupe being on TV. This time my dad didn't stop her.

Excitedly, Lupe and I got into the car. I thought we were just going to head over to the thrift store, but my mom said she was taking us to the mall.

"The trial's coming up soon, and you girls will need something nice to wear," she said. She took her credit card out from her wallet and flashed it with a grin. "We're going to JCPenney!"

"Woo-hoo!" Lupe and I shouted. It was about time I graduated from thrift store clothes!

Of course, we headed straight for the clearance racks. As we were searching, my mom's old friends walked over.

"Long time no see!" my mom greeted them in Mandarin. "Where have you guys been?"

"Oh, we tried to call you," Mrs. Zhao said, and the other wives nodded.

I knew this was a lie — I personally manned the phones, and even if she had tried to call while I was at school, our new phone system would have recorded it.

Still, my mom played along.

"I've been busy too," she said. "You know how it is."

The ladies pointed to Lupe.

"Who's she?" they asked. Lupe looked bashfully at them, poking me to translate.

"She's a friend of my daughter's," my mom replied. "A good family friend."

Mrs. Zhou raised a sharp eyebrow. "You have a lot of these kind of friends, don't you?" She frowned at Lupe.

"What do you mean?" my mom asked.

"*I* only let my daughter hang out with other Chinese kids," Mrs. Li told her.

"Me too," Mrs. Fang agreed. "It's better that way. This isn't the United Nations." She gave a little laugh.

I had heard more than enough. I tugged on my mom's hand, eager to leave. Forget JCPenney; I'd rather stick to my thrift shop.

Mrs. Zhou sighed at my mother. "I know you're fresh off the boat, so let me give you some advice," she said. "If you let your daughter hang out with Mexicans and blacks, she'll *xue huai*."

Xue huai means "learn bad" in Chinese. As soon as Mrs. Zhou said that, Mom burst out laughing. Then she looked straight at the three ladies and said, "The only danger my daughter has of *xue huai* is if she hangs out with you three bigots." She grabbed my hand and Lupe's. "C'mon, girls. Let's shop somewhere else."

We were just a few steps away, though, when my mom suddenly remembered. "Oh, and that man you saw me with? His name is

Hank. He's one of the finest people I know. Any of us would be *lucky* to be married to him."

Mrs. Li made a disgusted face. "Clearly you've been hanging out on the wrong side of the tracks, my friend."

My mom laughed again and said loudly in English, "You're not my friend! You're filled with toilet paper, just like the fake shopping bags I used to carry!"

Lupe and I giggled. I couldn't believe my mom was saying all these things! Go, Mom!

Just as we were about to walk out, I looked back at Mrs. Zhou's, Mrs. Li's, and Mrs. Fang's appalled faces—and stuck my tongue out at them.

My mom might have bright red lips and a new credit card, but deep down inside she was still the same person. I smiled. Clearly Dad and I weren't the only ones with *yi qi*!

CHAPTER 54

The sky on Election Day was stained with smoky gray clouds. After school, Lupe and I sat glued to the television. By the early evening, I could feel my eyeballs starting to melt. Lupe's mom called to tell Lupe that no matter what happened, it was going to be okay. To have faith. But by the time the moon rose high above the big Calivista sign, all the television reporters were saying Wilson was going to win.

I shook my head. "That can't be right," I said.

"What if it is?" Lupe asked, walking over and staring at the numbers up close before finally switching off the TV.

I'd been telling myself there was *no* way that Prop 187 was going to pass and looking for little signs to support this belief. And there were lots of little signs, like my letter being published in the newspaper, Ms. Patel agreeing to help Lupe's dad for free, the protestors outside the county jail, all the people at the march, and Mrs. Welch turning into a surprisingly good teacher.

But there were also lots and lots of signs that it *would* pass, like the poster at the pool, the flyers under the doors, the graffiti on the wall of the grocery store, the scribbles on the wall outside the bathroom at school, and the list of hate crimes as tall as our Calivista sign.

We'd heard on the news that if Prop 187 passed, there was going to be a lawsuit. I reminded Lupe of the powerful word *appeal* and what had happened with my mom's credit card rejection. But she shook her head.

"This is different," she said. "If it passes, Pete Wilson's not going to let the voters down."

The phone rang. Tomorrow was moving day for Jason's family, and he called to ask if I could come over and help him pack. I knew I should stay with Lupe through election night. But I also knew how stressful moving was, having done it a million times myself.

"Hey, Lupe, do you mind if I go over and help Jason move?" I asked.

She shrugged. "Sure," she said. "I can hang out with Hank. We won't know the results until tomorrow anyway."

When I got to Jason's house, Mrs. Yao was in the living room, instructing a team of packers how to carefully wrap up their expensive art. There were boxes everywhere.

"Oh, hi, Mia," she said, putting the jade vase she was carrying down and looking slightly embarrassed.

"Hi, Mrs. Yao." I stood there awkwardly. "Do you need any help?"

One of the movers came in and announced, "Ma'am, you're not going to be able to fit all this in your new house."

"Why not?" she asked, shaking her head curtly.

"Because it's half the size of this one."

Mrs. Yao's face turned steaming red, like it did the day at the motel when she yelled at Jason for picking up feathers. "It's none of your concern how to make it fit," she said, jabbing a box with her manicured finger. "You'll do as I say and pack it *all* up!"

I went to go find Jason. He was in his room, buried in a fort of Nerf guns, LEGOs, video game consoles, books, and clothes. His head poked out when I knocked.

"My mom says I can only take three boxes," he muttered. Then curled his body into a ball again and shrank down into the fort.

I looked over at the three empty boxes sitting in the corner, then at the mountain of stuff.

"I don't know how to decide," Jason admitted from his hiding place. "I want to take it all. . . ."

I recognized the fear in his voice, the worry that if he didn't take every single thing, a part of him would be lost forever. I walked over and squeezed in next to him. "You know," I said gently, "when I first moved to America, all I could bring was a tiny carry-on suitcase. I had to fit all my belongings into it."

Jason looked up, chewing his lip. "Really?"

I nodded.

"How'd you do it?" he asked.

I put a finger to my chin, recalling. "I played a little game called, *If you were stuck on an island and you could only bring one thing, what would it be?*"

"Definitely the *Joy of Cooking,*" Jason decided. "I gotta have my recipes."

I smiled and spotted the big cookbook in the pile. I picked it up, walked over, and put it inside one of the empty boxes. Then I asked Jason to pick one more item. He chose his chef's card from the cooking class. Then his video game console. Then he picked up a gold watch his dad had given him.

"This was my grandfather's," he said, handing it to me. "It's really special because he bought it with the money he made from running a Chinese restaurant. My dad called it sweat money."

I looked down at my own T-shirt and shorts, wondering if they were bought with sweat money too. I almost wanted to smell them. And did that make them less cool or more? More, I decided, because it meant we took extra care of them.

Carefully, I wrapped up the watch in tissue paper and put it into the box.

"What else?" I asked Jason.

We kept playing the Stuck on an Island game until all three moving boxes were packed. When the last one was sealed, we looked at all the toys and books and junk that hadn't made it. There was still a sizable toy pile in the middle of the room, enough to entertain a small village of kids.

"What do I do with the rest of it?" he asked.

"Why don't you bring it to the motel?" I suggested. "I bet some of the immigrants' kids who come on Wednesdays would love this!"

"Great idea!" Jason grinned. "Let's get some more boxes from the moving guys so we can pack them up!"

I beamed. As we walked out of his room to get the boxes, I spotted Mr. Yao in the living room. He was sitting on the cold, bare marble floor, the couch having already been wrapped and moved. In his lap was a thick stack of bills, and his fingers were punching numbers into a calculator. He looked so . . . small. It was a sharp difference from the first time I saw him in this very room, sitting atop his throne, oozing opulence and power. As I watched him, I started thinking about the two roller coasters again. I'd been so fixated on going from the poor one to the rich roller coaster, I never once thought about what it'd be like to go the other way around.

Mr. Yao caught me staring at him and snapped, "What are you looking at?"

"I—uh—I was just wondering, did you vote today?"

"Sure, I voted," he said. With a smug face, he announced, "I voted for Wilson and Prop 187."

Of course he did. Even when he was down, he somehow managed to kick someone else.

"How are you guys doing at the motel?" he asked.

"Good," I told him.

"Well, I wish I could say the same for me."

As he turned back to his bills, Mr. Yao let out one of those exasperated sighs my dad usually reserved for unflushed toilets in the guest rooms. It was almost enough to make me feel sorry for him.

It was late when I got back. Lupe was already asleep. My mom said Lupe didn't want to stay up to watch any more election coverage. I didn't blame her. She'd just talked to her mom on the phone and gone to sleep.

The motel was eerily quiet that night. The air, charged and heavy, sent the few customers hanging out in the parking lot back to their rooms. Every so often, I fought the urge to turn our TV on, to see who was winning, but I made myself go to bed early too.

As I crawled into bed next to Lupe, I closed my eyes and whispered, "Please don't let Prop 187 pass."

. . .

I woke up the next morning to bright, blazing sunshine and chirping birds. It *felt* like it was going to be a good day, the start of a new chapter. I glanced over at Lupe's bed. She wasn't there.

I jumped out of bed and threw on a sweatshirt. As I turned the doorknob, I hesitated for a second, readying myself for whatever news awaited me on the other side. *It's going to be okay. No matter what happened, it'll be okay.*

But nothing in the world could have prepared me for the sight I was about to see.

Lupe was in the kitchen, bent over my mom's lap, crying. Her knuckles were in her mouth. The newspaper was on the floor.

Proposition 187 had passed.

CHAPTER 55

The loud telephone ringing echoed in my ear. I walked over to get it, still in a daze of shock. It was Mrs. Garcia, reminding Lupe to stay home that day. Even though the news was saying that Prop 187 wasn't going to go into effect right away, Lupe's mom insisted it was too risky to go to school, and my mom agreed. So Lupe stayed with Hank and my parents, and I walked to school alone.

In class, I stared at her empty seat while Mrs. Welch took roll. In addition to Lupe, Hector, Rosa, and Jorge were also absent. Stuart raised his hand and immediately asked whether this meant they were undocumented. Mrs. Welch snapped at him, "That is none of your concern."

It was, though, the concern of a majority of Californians. In the end, it wasn't even close. Wilson had won by fifteen points, and Prop 187 passed by an even larger margin—60 percent to 40 percent. Sixty percent. That was how many Californians had no problem pulling Lupe out of school.

At lunch, I waited for the Kids for Kids club to show up to the trailer classroom. Most were absent, though, and the few who did come, once they saw how few people there were, left and went back to the cafeteria. I sat alone in the empty trailer classroom, trying not to think this was it—the club I'd started was gone.

The door opened and I looked over. It was Jason.

"Where's Lupe?" he asked. "I have to tell her something."

"She can't come to school anymore, because of Prop 187, remember?" I said. And just because I was so mad and frustrated at the election results, I threw in, "Thanks to your dad."

"Hey! That's not fair."

I crossed my arms. "Well, he voted for it!"

"Yeah, but he's one person!"

"Still," I muttered.

Jason threw up his hands. "You know what? I came over to say that I told my mom what she did to Lupe and her mom was not cool. But I'm starting to think it doesn't matter what I do. You guys are never going to separate me from my parents!"

He walked out, banging the door, leaving me all alone with my soggy corn dog. I wished Lupe was there to make me feel better. But as I looked around the empty trailer classroom, it felt like the first day of school all over again, and I didn't know a single soul.

CHAPTER 56

Lupe and my mom were standing in front of the big palm tree on the side of the pool when I got home. There weren't a lot of immigrants for Mrs. T's How to Navigate America class that day — most had called and canceled in the morning, saying they were too shocked and saddened by the passage of 187 to come out. So Mom was teaching Lupe by herself. The afternoon sun stretched their shadows across the pavement.

"Your mom's teaching me how to use shadows to measure proportions," Lupe said. Then she bent down with her measuring tape and started measuring my shadow too. I stood up as straight as I could.

"That's so neat," I said.

"I also learned about the x axis and the y axis," Lupe added.

Wow. That was more than I'd learned in math that day.

"Lupe's a great student," my mom said proudly.

"And you're a great math teacher," my dad said, walking over. She beamed.

Hank joined us and put his hand on Lupe's shoulder. "Your mom's calling for you from Mexico," he told her.

Lupe left, and I walked with Hank to the supplies room, grabbing us some sodas and telling him all about my fight with Jason.

"You know his dad voted for Prop 187?" Every time I thought about it, it made my fingers stiffen. Mr. Yao voted to kick my best friend out of school. *My* best friend.

"But *Jason* didn't," Hank reminded me.

I took a sip of my soda. "Still. It just makes me so mad."

Hank reached for a new box of toilet paper. "I know. But you can't give up on people. It's one of the three keys of friendship. You gotta listen, you gotta care, and most importantly, you gotta keep trying. Jason's not the same as his parents."

"I know, but . . ." I squeezed my eyes shut, thinking of all the dinner conversations I'd have to endure at his house if I ever went over there again. Having to talk to Mr. Yao, all the while knowing *what he did.* "I don't know if I'm strong enough," I admitted.

Hank let out a hearty laugh as he sat down on the chair in the supplies room. "*You,* not strong enough? You were strong enough to buy the motel from Yao. You were strong when business fell. You were strong enough to stand up to Mr. Cooper — even I thought we should have caved *that* time. And when your teacher said you couldn't write, what did you do? You went out and became a *published* writer!" With a twinkle in his eye, Hank added, "You're stronger than you think, Mia Tang."

Well, when he put it like *that.*

"I think you can handle being Jason's friend," Hank said, putting a hand on my shoulder. "Remember what I told you that day at the park? I'm sure that through your small interactions, you'll inspire him to be a better person than his parents."

Hank and his wise words had helped me so much with

Mrs. Welch. You'd think I'd have known it by now. But sometimes, you just needed to hear a thing twice.

. . .

I fidgeted in my seat while Mrs. Welch spent recess trying to teach me how to analyze literature. We had moved on from the beginner stuff to motifs and themes and characterization. She was teaching me things the other kids weren't learning yet. It was interesting, and I appreciated the challenge, but today my mind was elsewhere.

Mrs. Welch waved her hands at me. "Hello? Earth to Mia! Are you listening?"

"Huh?"

She sat down beside me. "What's wrong?" she asked.

What was wrong was I was sitting here practically getting a private literature class from a college professor, when my best friend wasn't even allowed to go to school. And I hadn't been able to find Jason all day. And most of the Kids for Kids members were still not back in school.

My eyes started tearing up, and I blinked furiously so Mrs. Welch couldn't see.

"Are the concepts too hard?" she went on. "Do you want me to slow down?"

I shook my head. "That's not it," I said.

"Then what is it?"

Mrs. Welch followed my gaze over to Lupe's empty desk. She put her book down and asked me softly, "How's she doing?"

I didn't want to say anything. I didn't want to get Lupe in trouble, especially now.

"Her dad's trial is in two weeks, isn't it?"

I looked up in surprise. "How'd you know?"

"Lupe told me when I came by the motel. She asked me to write her a letter of support for the hearing," she said.

I sat up. *She did?* My mind flashed back to the two of them chatting in the parking lot while my mom was teaching. So that's what Lupe was talking to her about.

Mrs. Welch walked over to her desk and picked up a sealed envelope and handed it to me. I gazed down at it, so surprised and impressed that Lupe found the courage to ask, and Mrs. Welch found the kindness to say yes.

"Tell Lupe we miss her. And she can come back anytime."

"But Prop 187 —"

"The courts have stopped it for now. No one is going to report her," Mrs. Welch promised. She paused and added, "And even if the courts weren't blocking it . . . I still wouldn't report her. You have my word."

As I took the letter from Mrs. Welch, I thought about how different she was from the first day of class. I would never have believed then that Prop 187 would actually pass — or that Mrs. Welch would offer her word not to follow it. I guess Wilson convinced a lot of people, but there were a couple of people I unconvinced myself.

CHAPTER 57

Lupe was overjoyed when I gave her Mrs. Welch's letter and message that she could come back to school.

"But I'm going to miss your mom's lessons," Lupe said as we got all our documents and petitions ready to take to Ms. Patel that weekend. We were meeting her at her office one final time before the trial. "She sure is a good math teacher." Her eyes flashed. "She should be a *real* math teacher!"

"But then who's going to clean the rooms?" I reminded Lupe. "I don't think we have enough money to hire an additional cleaning person."

My eyes slid over to the pile of uncleaned rooms' keys sitting on the front desk, and next to them, the technical certification books my dad had borrowed from the library. He hadn't had time to open any of them. They'd just been gathering dust.

Just then, we heard a scream from Mrs. Q's room. Lupe and I rushed out the back and found her pointing at her television.

"A twelve-year-old boy was just pronounced dead in Anaheim, California," the newscaster announced. "His name was Julio, and his parents, who are illegal immigrants, said he got sick earlier this week, but they delayed getting him medical treatment because they feared Proposition 187 would require the hospital to deport them."

"Oh my God. . . ." I said. Lupe sank down on the floor.

"Early autopsy results indicate that the boy had an infection. By the time the fire department arrived, it was too late. He wasn't breathing and his heart stopped," the reporter continued. "His parents said they were afraid of the consequences of going to the hospital."

Lupe rocked her body back and forth. Mrs. Q tried to scoop her up, but this time, Lupe wiggled away. "I want my parents. I want my parents," she said over and over again.

. . .

Lupe was trying to dial her mom when Jason came into the front office. I looked up from the newspaper article talking about how the tragedy had hit Anaheim deep and many local residents were stopping by Julio's apartment building and laying down flowers.

"I saw the news," he said. "I couldn't just sit at home and do nothing, so I made this." He presented a plate of toasted quesadillas, the cheese perfectly grilled and glistening under the fluorescent front desk lights. "Will you go with me, Lupe, to give them to Julio's mother?"

He picked up one of the quesadillas and offered it to her. "They're mushroom with teriyaki."

Lupe gazed at the food and slowly put down the phone.

"That's nice of you," she said.

As she went to go grab her jacket, I apologized to Jason.

"I'm not my father, you know," he said.

I nodded as our eyes locked. He'd been trying to tell me all year. More importantly, he'd been trying to *show* me.

"I know."

CHAPTER 58

Mrs. T and Mrs. Q's class next Wednesday was standing room only as immigrants of all different ethnicities and backgrounds flocked to our motel, many of them sick and afraid to go to the hospital.

As my mom gathered up the little ones and got them started on some math games, Lupe and I went from person to person, explaining to them what Ms. Patel told us. Though Prop 187 passed, there was a court injunction, meaning it couldn't be enforced until the courts said it was legal. A process that could take years.

"In the meantime, it's safe to go to school and the hospital," Lupe emphasized.

I repeated the same thing in Chinese for the Chinese aunties and uncles.

But the aunties and uncles looked warily at us, like they didn't trust our words. They trusted what they saw: A child had *died*.

"What do we do?" Lupe asked me.

I went and got my dad. When he saw the sick immigrants, he immediately opened up five more rooms so they'd be more comfortable. Then he started calling his friends — all the ones who had been doctors in China, plus Mrs. Morales, the nurse from Mexico, and other Latino immigrants we knew who used to work in the medical profession back home. They came over, and with their help, we set up a clinic right there at the Calivista.

As Lupe and I brought in the patients and helped translate, my dad asked his friends, who had recently passed the required licensing exams in California, what it was like to work at a hospital or a lab instead of at a restaurant or a motel.

"It feels . . ." His friends' chests swelled. "Like we've arrived."

My dad nodded as his friends turned their attention back to the patients. They didn't see him dabbing his eye, but I did. I realized then, there were some things my parents gave up that they could never get back, even though we were making more money. Like the ability to do what they truly wanted.

• • •

At school, even though Lupe had come back right after Mrs. Welch told her she could, some kids were still absent, like Rosa and Jorge. Still, we carried on with the lunch meeting of Kids for Kids. Our top club priority was making a final push to get more signatures for José's petition! Lupe's dad's trial was less than a week away!

All week, we'd been making last-minute phone calls. We now had 872 signatures and five politicians who were publicly throwing their support behind José. We were so proud of what we'd achieved. It was a tremendous effort, more than we ever thought we'd be able to accomplish. But was it enough?

• • •

The night before the hearing, my stomach was in a bundle, wound tighter than the sheets in the washing machine.

"If I have to go back to Mexico, will you visit me?" Lupe asked as we both lay awake in bed.

"You're not going anywhere," I assured her.

Lupe sat up. "Mia! I have to be prepared!"

I turned onto my stomach. "No, you don't," I insisted. Why did she have to prepare for things that didn't need preparing for?

But Lupe was an over-planner. "If my dad gets deported, both my parents will be back in Mexico. I'll have to go back; I can't stay here by myself."

"You wouldn't stay here by yourself," I muttered to the sheets. "You have me, remember?"

Lupe reached out from the rollaway bed with her hand. "I can't be separated from my parents, Mia," she said. "I just can't." Her voice wobbled slightly, and I clung to her fingers. Of course she couldn't, just like I couldn't be separated from mine. No matter how hard things got for my family, it was always better when we were together.

"You're not going to get separated from your parents," I promised. "Everything is going to work out. You'll see."

As Lupe drifted to sleep, I looked out the window at the soft crescent moon and the bright stars blinking in the velvet night. It used to comfort me that they were the same stars my cousin Shen was looking at back in China. Tonight, I wondered if Lupe's mom was looking up at them too, praying and hoping she'd see her daughter soon.

I hoped tomorrow would bring good news for their family. I hoped it would bring change and kindness and decency. Most of all, I hoped, as I glanced over at Lupe sleeping soundly, that I wouldn't lose my first and only best friend in the world.

CHAPTER 59

We took three cars to the hearing—I went with Lupe in Hank's car, Fred and Billy Bob took another, and Mrs. T and Mrs. Q went with my parents in their car. Hank tried to make small talk as he drove, but Lupe and I were too nervous to keep up our part of the conversation. My nerves were like ice cubes, jiggling around inside me.

We slowed as we got closer, and I saw dozens of people standing on the courthouse steps carrying signs. Except they weren't the same signs people had been carrying outside the jail. These said *No Illegals!* and *Go back to where you came from!*

Lupe's knees began to shake.

"Ignore them," Hank said as he parked.

I gazed at the tall courthouse bumping its head into the clouds. I hoped the thick cement walls would shield the people inside from the loud chanting of the protestors outside.

Hank got out of the car and straightened his suit pants. We were all wearing our nicest clothes. Lupe had on a new blue skirt and red shirt, and I was wearing a new white dress. My mom had gone and picked them out for us at Mervyn's. We looked like we were going to a party, not a deportation hearing, but Ms. Patel had said it was important we looked good.

Hank took Lupe's hand and led her up the steps to the courthouse. As we walked, I could hear people chanting, "GO HOME! We don't want you here!" Louder and louder they chanted.

Hank leaned over and whispered, "Keep walking. Do *not* look at them." I reached over and grabbed Lupe's other freezing hand, and together we made our way into the courthouse. My eyes slid down to the legs of the protestors.

Once inside, a security guard asked us to put our things through a metal detector. He was a white guy, a bit older than Hank, with thinning hair and sad gray eyes. As he scanned Hank's wallet and my backpack, he kept looking at Lupe. I wanted to yell, "Can't you see she's going through a hard time?" But as he scanned her bag and handed it back to her, he whispered, "Good luck today."

Lupe smiled at him, gripping her backpack tightly. "Thanks," she said.

"Lupe! Mia!" Ms. Patel called. "C'mon. The hearing's about to start!"

The courtroom was filled with people. Some turned and glared at us, while others smiled. Lupe took a seat in the front row reserved for us, right behind where her dad and Ms. Patel were sitting. I sat down next to her. José wasn't there yet—they were bringing him over from the county jail. I opened my backpack and gave Ms. Patel our petition—at final count, we'd gotten all the way up to 927 signatures!

The side door opened, and José walked in. He was wearing a suit, which Hank and my mom had brought from his house. It looked good on him. José walked over to us, smiling and reaching out to Lupe. The two of them hugged and hugged. It must have felt so good to finally touch her dad after all these weeks and not have the glass partition separating them. José shook hands with Hank and my dad.

"All rise!" the bailiff called. I looked up and saw a tall man in a black robe walk in.

We all stood up.

. . .

Judge Hughes was just how I imagined him to be: old, white, and serious, just like the judges on the afternoon TV shows. He had the kind of poker face that my dad said made it hard to tell whether a person was going to check out early or check out late.

As Ms. Patel presented José's case, using terms like *cancellation of removal* and *deferred action status*, Judge Hughes neither nodded nor frowned.

"This is a man who has contributed substantially to the California economy," Ms. Patel said, nodding at José. "With the money he and his wife earned, they put it right back into their *home* state, investing in a motel in Anaheim, California."

Ms. Patel approached the bench to hand Judge Hughes the purchase papers for the motel as well as the letter from Mrs. Welch, attesting to the fact that Lupe was in school in Anaheim and that she was doing wonderfully well, showing particular promise in math and art.

"Deporting this man would mean separating him from his only child," she said. Lupe's chin trembled as she listened to Ms. Patel describe the possibility of tearing her dad away from her. I looked over at her and felt my own eyes watering. José turned around and held his daughter as she cried. There was a collective *awwww* in the room, and I turned around to see people in the audience dabbing their eyes and struggling to control their own emotions, including my mom and dad.

"For these reasons, we strongly urge this court to cancel José Garcia's deportation," Ms. Patel said. "We have the support of Senator Diane Feinstein, four assembly members, and one state senator, as well as a petition signed by over nine hundred people."

Ms. Patel handed over the stack of paper with all the signatures we'd gathered, and Judge Hughes took some time to look over it all. I scrutinized his face for signs, reading into every nose twitch and blink.

"Thank you," the judge finally said. He turned to the other side. "Does opposing counsel have anything they would like to add?"

The lawyer on the other side stood up.

"I would beg your honor to please think about the precedent we are setting here. The law is the law. While the circumstances are very moving and we are grateful to Mr. Garcia for his labor and work, if we allow Mr. Garcia to stay, then what about the next illegal immigrant? And the next? We must honor the law, even if it is difficult, or the law becomes meaningless."

Lupe squeezed my hand. I looked over at José, who was staring down into his miraculous cable-repairing hands. We were really going to need a miracle now.

As Judge Hughes cleared his voice to deliver his verdict, we all leaned forward and held our breaths.

"Thank you, counselors, for your speeches. This is not an easy case. It weighs upon me heavily to tear a father away from a child or to turn a blind eye to a violation of our laws. I would like to reiterate to all in this room, it is a violation of United States law to enter this country illegally. For those reasons, I'm afraid I'm going to have to deny the cancellation of removal."

The courtroom erupted. "This is outrageous!" Hank shouted.

"I'm not finished!" Judge Hughes shouted. "ORDER IN THE COURT!"

As Judge Hughes banged his gavel and demanded we all settle down, Lupe looked over at me. I could see the hope drain from her eyes. The pain broke my heart into a thousand pieces.

"Opposing side is right to say that if we ignore the law," Judge Hughes went on, "the law becomes meaningless. So I cannot cancel the order of removal today, I'm afraid. However." He paused for a beat, during which the entire room stopped breathing. Lupe glanced up. She put her hands together, sitting on the edge of her seat. "The law also requires that we weigh the totality of circumstances. And while it is true that Mr. Garcia broke the law, he has also committed no crimes while he has been here. He has been here for *eight years* and made this state his home. He has worked hard and raised a daughter, for whom it would be a tragedy to separate from her father, or to pull her from her home base here in the great state of California."

My heart lurched to my throat as I leaned in. *Does that mean . . . ?*

"And so it is that I am granting Mr. Garcia a *temporary* stay of removal. Mr. Garcia, you are free to go home with your daughter until such time as this court decides to reopen and reevaluate your immigration case. This court is adjourned." And with that, Judge Hughes brought down his gavel again.

"OH MY GOD!" Lupe exclaimed, throwing her arms around her dad. "Papi! Did you hear that?"

All the weeklies and my parents cheered as José shook Ms. Patel's hand and gave her a hug, his voice choking with emotion as he thanked her and asked if she needed any help with her cable.

"I'm good," Ms. Patel replied, chuckling. She turned to us, serious. "I know we didn't get exactly what we wanted on the first try. But trust me, guys, this is a *huge* step in the right direction. José isn't going anywhere, and in six months, when we come back to present our case, I'm going to hit them with everything I've got." She looked into José's eyes. "I'm going to fight for you, and I'm not going to stop until you and your family get to stay for good."

As Judge Hughes got up from the bench to leave the room, we all turned to him. I raised my hand. This time, I didn't wait to be called on.

"Thank you, Judge," I called out. Judge Hughes looked over at us and nodded.

· · ·

Lupe's mom cried when she heard her husband's voice on the phone. It was the first time they'd spoken since José had been arrested. José told her the good news, along with Ms. Patel's advice that Lupe's mom stay in Mexico until the new court date. There was a good chance the judge would grant his cancellation of removal at the next court hearing, and if so, she could come back legally.

Still, six months was a long time. As Lupe struggled with the thought of not seeing her mom for six more months, my dad had an idea. He suggested Lupe and José move into one of the rooms at the Calivista.

"Can we, Dad?" Lupe asked.

"Well . . ." José hesitated. "It's still going to be hard without your mom."

I slipped my hand in Lupe's and smiled at José.

"But at least you'll be surrounded by family."

CHAPTER 60

We had a party the next day in the Kids for Kids club. I brought cans of cream soda from the vending machine in my backpack, and Lupe brought chips. As I passed them out, Jason came up and congratulated Lupe.

"I'm so glad they let your dad stay!" he said, throwing his arms around her.

"It's just for now," she told him as she hugged him back. "But thanks."

I could tell she was trying to manage her expectations, but in my mind, it was practically a done deal.

"Trust me, we're gonna win for good in six months," I said confidently.

Lupe grinned. "If that happens, we're *definitely* going to Disneyland!"

We started giggling uncontrollably, then stopped when we saw Jason's face. He was staring down at his shoes. I noticed he'd recently switched from wearing pricey Air Jordans to plain gray Converses. "I hope my parents let me go," he said. "My cooking classes are already kind of expensive, though. . . ."

I had an idea. "If they don't, I know a park where we can watch the Disneyland fireworks. It'd be just like we're at Disneyland — and it's totally free!"

Jason's face brightened. "That sounds great! I can make us a picnic!" He smiled at Lupe. "Congratulations again," he said. "I don't know how you stayed so strong at the trial. If it were me, I would have crumbled."

"No, you wouldn't," I said.

Jason wriggled uncomfortably. "My dad makes all the money in our house. If they ever took him . . . I don't know what we'd do."

Get a job? But I didn't say that. Instead, I looked into his eyes and told him what Hank said about me. "You're stronger than you think, Jason Yao."

Jason smiled.

Later in class, Mrs. Welch wrote a math question on the board:

A man bought a bicycle for $50. He made $28 worth of improvements on it. He can sell his improved bicycle for $86. Assuming he wants to make the most profit, should he sell his bicycle, and how much profit can he make?

Lupe raised her hand. I smiled. Ever since she got back, she's been on fire, answering question after question.

"Yes, Lupe?" Mrs. Welch said.

"Besides selling his bike, can he rent it out?" she asked.

My classmates put their pencils down. I could see the lightbulb going off in their heads, like, *Oh, yeahhhh!*

"That's a very good question," Mrs. Welch said. She thought it over and declared, "Let's assume yes, he can rent out the bike for . . . thirty dollars a day."

"Then I think he should keep it. Thirty dollars a day is a lot of money," Lupe said, glancing at me. "You can get yourself a nice room at our motel for that, right, Mia?"

I beamed. It was the first time she called it *our* motel, not just in the club but in class. "Yup!" I said.

"And if he rents it *twice* a day, that's sixty dollars!" Lupe added.

"Or ninety dollars if he rents it three times!" Stuart jumped in.

"One hundred twenty dollars if he rents it four times!" I added.

Dillon Fischer, who always had to have the last word, chimed in, "Seven hundred twenty dollars if he rents it out every hour!"

Mrs. Welch held up her hands. "All right, all right, I get the idea." She chuckled. She had a lot more patience than in the beginning of the school year. "What can I say? You guys are a smart bunch," she said, smiling.

. . .

As we walked home from school, I complimented Lupe on her quick thinking.

"Thanks," she said. "I wish there was some way we could rent *our* rooms out twice a day."

"That would be amazing. We could make twice as much money." I giggled. "But rooms aren't bikes. People have to sleep through the night. And there's only one night, so . . ."

Lupe thought about that, then asked, "What if we added more beds?"

She was joking, right? But she had this look on her face, the same look my mom got whenever she spotted a really good deal on jasmine rice when we went to 99 Ranch. "No, think about it! We have thirty rooms, right?"

"Right. . . ."

"And we're charging twenty dollars a night. What if we split them or put bunk beds in the rooms and charged people ten dollars a night?" Her eyes widened, and she covered her mouth. "*That's* how we can get the profits back up!!*"*

"You want to put bunk beds in all the rooms?" I asked. I wasn't so sure if that was such a good idea.

Lupe sat down on the curb and pulled out her pencil case and her drawing pad—and started drawing out *math*! I watched as Lupe sketched out all thirty Calivista rooms, each with two sets of bunk beds in them, and jotted down numbers next to them.

"So you're saying if we put bunk beds in the rooms, we could have four beds per room and charge people ten dollars a bed, instead of twenty dollars. Let's see, four times ten . . . that's forty dollars a room, instead of twenty dollars," I said. Holy cow.

My eyes bulged—that would *double* the profit! I stared back at Lupe, who looked totally relaxed, just sitting there kicking it on the curb, squinting at the sun, like it was an ordinary day and she hadn't just come up with a way to completely transform our business!

"You are a genius!" I said to Lupe, jumping to my feet and pulling her up.

The two of us ran all the way back to the motel.

CHAPTER 61

When Hank heard Lupe's plan, he clapped his hands.

"It's brilliant, just brilliant!" he said.

We sat in the living room of the manager's quarters while my dad crunched the numbers on his calculator. "But how are we going to afford all the bunk beds?" he asked.

Hank grinned and reached for the phone. "This is *exactly* why I got the line of credit! Precisely for moments like this!"

As Hank waited on the line for the banker, my mom rubbed her hands excitedly together. "Just think, if we truly doubled our profits, maybe we'd finally have enough money to hire someone to help us clean. Wouldn't that be amazing?"

A whimsical smile played on my dad's lips as he reached a hand to his achy shoulder.

. . .

The day before Thanksgiving, the delivery guys carried the beds inside the rooms as Billy Bob and Fred helped my parents change the price on the big sign overhead from *$20/night* to *$10/ night*.

"At those rates, you can't afford *not* to stay here," Hank said with a hearty laugh, admiring the sign.

"Remember, this will only work if we pack them in," Lupe

reminded us. "If we only put one or two people in a room, it won't work. We need volume, people!"

I smiled at her. Spoken like a real businesswoman.

. . .

Lured by our bright neon sign, the new customers came in droves. They were students, immigrants, young couples traveling on a budget, and truck drivers who just needed a place to crash for a few hours before they hit the road again. We packed them four to a room, just as Lupe had envisioned.

By the end of the long weekend, Mr. Cooper and the other investors were happy that the profits were up again, and my dad even asked me to write a *HELP WANTED* sign and put it on the window. I sat at the front desk, drawing with a ruler and a black permanent marker. When I was done, I went out the back to show my dad the sign.

I found him in the laundry room, sitting next to the pyramid of crushed recycling cans he was sorting — now that there were more customers, there were a LOT more soda cans too. In his lap were the books that he had borrowed from the library.

"Hey, Dad," I said, smiling down at his books. Maybe now that he could get some help with the cleaning, he'd finally have time to go through the books. "Are you studying to be a lab technician?"

My dad chuckled. "Nope. I'm just looking at these one last time before I return them," he said.

"*Return* them? Why?"

He gestured toward the piles and piles of dirty towels scattered around the laundry room, as if to say, *That's why.*

"But we're going to hire someone to help with all of that," I told him. I held up my new *HELP WANTED* sign.

My dad smiled and said the sign looked great. Then he patted the small wooden stool next to him. I took a seat.

"Even if we hire someone else, it's still not enough for your mom and me to both go after our dreams," he said with a sigh. "Sometimes in families, you can only choose one."

He reached down and touched the cover of his lab technician certificate book with his calloused hands one last time, before reluctantly putting it away.

"And I'm choosing your mom's."

. . .

When my dad got back from the library, he had a new book, which he gently placed in my mom's lap. She was in the middle of making a bunch of new keys for all the additional customers. My mom was so shocked when she saw the book, she nearly made a key out of her sweater.

High School Math Licensing Exam, it said on the spine.

"I was thinking with the additional cleaning staff, we don't both have to clean all day," my dad said. "I think you should go for it. You're an amazing teacher!"

My mom was speechless. She got up and hugged my dad as the keys in her lap fell on the floor.

"Thank you for seeing me," she said, tearfully. "Even if I don't pass the exam—"

My dad put his hands on my mom's arms. "Oh, you'll pass," he chuckled. He turned to me and asked, "Have you *ever* seen your mom not accomplish what she put her mind to?"

I thought of all the little things my mom did to get what she wanted — the fake shopping bags, the free sample perfumes, the beet juice she dabbed on her lips when she couldn't afford lipstick. My mom *always* found a way.

"You'll pass, Mom," I said.

She laughed and gave us both a big hug.

CHAPTER 62

"Are you ready?" Lupe asked.

It was the big day we'd all been waiting for — the official grand opening of the Calivista Hostel Motel! Even though technically we'd been open for a week already, today was the day of our official grand opening, and we were inviting all our investors and old customers to come celebrate.

I nodded and told Lupe I'd be right there — as soon as I finished hanging up the last of the framed copies of my Letter to the Editor on the wall. There was one in each of the guest rooms, along with framed copies of Lupe's landscapes. But the room I was the *proudest* of hanging up my published writing was in the laundry room, where I knew my dad spent the most time. I wanted him to be able to look up at my writing every night as he folded the towels. He wasn't just picking my mom's dreams. He was picking mine too.

Lupe and Jason were in the manager's quarters when I got back. Lupe was in a brand-new yellow dress that José got her from Sears, and Jason was wearing a chef's apron and hat. He was the official caterer today, and he was making one of his new recipes that he'd learned from his cooking class. Jason ran around my mom's kitchen, putting the finishing touches on the hors d'oeuvres for the big party like a real chef.

"Mango pot stickers!" he announced proudly, presenting us with a plate of sweet and tangy dumplings fried to golden perfection. I took a dumpling and bit into it. The gooey mango melted in my mouth.

"Jason, this is delicious!" I said.

He smiled. Outside, the guests were starting to arrive. Lupe and I each grabbed a plate of dumplings and headed out.

"Mom, c'mon, it's time!" I called. She closed the math licensing exam book that she'd been reading nonstop and went into the bathroom to change. She came out wearing a bright pink sundress she'd bought on sale at Ross.

"You look beautiful," my dad said. He marveled at her, standing proud and tall in his pair of black slacks, a crisp white shirt, and a gray sports jacket that he'd borrowed from Hank. My mom slipped her arm in his.

"You were right about the clearance rack," my mom said to him with a smile. "There's a lot of good stuff in there!"

Outside, there was a long line of cars waiting to pull into the Calivista. Most of the guests were gathered at the pool, mingling. I spotted Mr. Abayan, Auntie Ling, Mr. Bhagawati, and many of our other shareholders. Even Mrs. Welch was there! As my mom and dad went over to say hi to everyone, Lupe and I walked around with plates of dumplings.

"This is so nice!" the investors said, nodding at the walls we'd gotten freshly painted the week before.

I felt a tap on my shoulder and turned around to see Mr. and Mrs. Yao.

"We were in the neighborhood," Mr. Yao said to me. He

waved at José, standing over at the grill next to Hank. José gave him a little wave back. Then Mr. Yao turned to Lupe. "I heard the news about your dad. I'm glad they let him stay. He was a good worker."

"Your mom too," Mrs. Yao added. She put a hand on Lupe's arm. "I, uh . . . I owe you an apology."

Mrs. Yao and Lupe went to find a quiet place to talk, leaving Mr. Yao and I standing alone by the pool. I offered him one of Jason's dumplings. At first, Mr. Yao shook his head, but when I insisted he try it and bet him five dollars he'd like it, he popped one in his mouth.

"*Mmm*, these are tasty," Mr. Yao agreed as he munched on the pot sticker. He reached for another one, but my plate was empty. I hollered at Jason to get his dad some more, and Jason grinned so hard, his cheeks dimpled.

As Mr. Yao waited for the dumplings, he gazed around at the pool and the rooms. I thought maybe he was a bit sad seeing his motel get turned into a hostel, but instead, he said, "Congratulations, Mia. Very well done."

He held out his hand.

I can't describe the feelings that coursed through me as I shook Mr. Yao's hand. Why did it mean *so much* to me to finally hear him say that? After all this time, everything I'd been through, why did I still care what he thought? But I did. For some unexplainable reason, that day, as I took Mr. Yao's hand and shook it, I felt myself come full circle as a manager.

The skin around his eyes stretched as he offered me a rare smile.

Just then I heard Hank's voice calling across the pool. "Mia! Get over here! We're ready to cut the ribbon!"

I turned to see Hank waving a big pair of golden scissors.

"Excuse me," I said to Mr. Yao, then walked over to the front office and joined Hank, Lupe, José, my parents, and the weeklies.

As Lupe held out the red ribbon and Jason lifted up the bow, I cut it with the golden scissors. The entire motel erupted in cheers.

"To the new Calivista!"

Lupe, Jason, and I threw our arms around one another, our laughter jingling like three keys on a ring.

AUTHOR'S NOTE

I was ten years old when Proposition 187 passed. That year, I watched in horror as the advertisements blasted on television and my Latino friends hung their heads in shame, huddled in the back of the classroom. The boy who died. Julio Cano,[1] was just two years older than me and lived in the same town.

I remember as a child watching my best friends — many of whom were Mexican and came from blended families — worry about whether they and their family members would be next. The anger and vitriol directed at illegal immigration was everywhere, this explosive rage that you could feel when you walked down the street. In school, kids would point and whisper whenever a child who wasn't white walked past, speculating whether they were illegal — their voices soft at first, and then louder and louder as it got closer to the election.

And then on that Election Day in 1994, I remember watching as people cheered when it was announced that Proposition 187 had passed — 60 to 40.[2] The knowledge that that many Californians

1. Lee Romney and Julie Marquis, "Activists Cite Boy's Death as First Prop. 187 Casualty," *Los Angeles Times*, November 23, 1994, http://articles.latimes.com/1994 -11-23/news/mn-689_1_illegal-immigrant-parents.
2. David E. Early and Josh Richman, "Twenty Years After Prop. 187, Attitudes Toward Illegal Immigration Have Changed Dramatically in California," *Mercury*

voted to not allow innocent children to go to school made me sick to my stomach. It was a permanent and irreversible slap across the face to me and every immigrant I knew.

Later that year, we moved to Chula Vista, California, a border town, just eight miles from Mexico. I made friends with many other fellow immigrant children and witnessed the traumatizing effects of Prop 187 on their families, the lingering fear and worry and anxiety of the provisions, even as Prop 187 was being legally challenged.

I carried these memories with me for many, many years, until one day, I was sitting in a political science class in college. The professor was a man from TV that I recognized—Governor Pete Wilson's campaign spokesman, Dan Schnur. I was taking a class with one of the masterminds of Wilson's campaign. That semester, the distress and frustration of my childhood all came flooding back as I listened to the strategy behind the pain I had witnessed.[3] To get through the course, I reminded myself it was in the past. Prop 187 had been struck down by the courts. We'd moved on. No candidate in the future would ever try to pull something like that again.

I was wrong.

In the summer of 2015, I watched as presidential candidate Donald Trump got on TV and blasted Mexicans as criminals. It was like déjà vu—the same anger, hate, and vitriol, a punch from

News, November 22, 2014, http://www.mercurynews.com/2014/11/22/twenty-years-after-prop-187-attitudes-toward-illegal-immigration-have-changed-dramatically-in-california.

3. Dan Schnur described the strategy behind the 1994 Pete Wilson Campaign at the Institute of Governmental Studies conference on the 1994 Gubernatorial Election, a transcript of which was published in *California Votes: The 1994 Governor's Race: An Inside Look at the Candidates and Their Campaigns by the People Who Managed Them*, edited by Gerald Lubenow (Berkeley: Institute of Governmental Studies Press, 1995).

the past, a page directly out of Wilson's playbook. Like Wilson, Trump rode that anger all the way to victory. In the years that followed, President Trump separated immigrant children from their parents at the border. The number of deportations of undocumented immigrants with no prior criminal records has tripled under Trump.[4]

This time, I knew I had to write about it.

In my research for this story, I visited an immigration detention jail, spoke at length to immigration lawyers, interviewed families, and conducted extensive research on the 1994 election, including the sharp increase in hate crimes in the months before and after Proposition 187 passed. Every single one of the hate crimes depicted in this novel actually happened during this period in California history. According to 1990 census data, one in four California residents were Latino.[5] In the eleven months following the passage of Prop 187, there were thousands of instances of harassment and rights abuses committed against Latinos in Southern California. The Los Angeles County Commission on Human Relations recorded a 24 percent increase in hate crimes against Latinos in 1994 and 1995. Among them, many Latinos were turned away from banks, refused service, told to "go back to where you come from," and forced to show their money before ordering in restaurants. Latinos in North Hollywood were asked

4. Rogue Planas and Elise Foley, "Deportations of Noncriminals Rise as ICE Casts Wider Net," *HuffPost*, updated January 9, 2018, https://www.huffingtonpost.com/entry/trump-immigration-deportation-noncriminals_us_5a25dfc8e4b07324e8401714.
5. Mark Baldassare, *A California State of Mind: The Conflicted Voter in a Changing World* (Berkeley: University of California Press, 2002), 151.

by bus drivers to pay more than non-Latino riders — often double the regular fare — and asked to sit at the back of the bus. An apartment manager of a Van Nuys apartment building told a Latina woman — a citizen — that she and her children could not use the pool after 6:00 p.m., because those hours were for "whites only." A Los Angeles woman was viciously bitten by a dog, and when she asked the owner to help with the medical bill, he responded, "Illegals have no right to medical care, Pete Wilson said so." In October 1994, an Inglewood police officer arrived at the home of a legal permanent resident and drew his weapon because he said her stereo was on too loud. He threatened to deport her to Mexico if he ever had to come back.[6]

In schools, teachers assigned students to write essays about their parents' immigration status.[7] After Proposition 187 passed, in addition to Julio Cano dying, some hospitals and clinics reported a sharp decline in patients. In the weeks and months after Prop 187 passed, there were also reports that some of the estimated 300,000 to 400,000 undocumented children in California schools were not going to school.[8]

In addition to quantitative research, I also conducted qualitative research. I spent time in the Central Valley interviewing blended and undocumented families, migrant workers, and field workers, to

6. Nancy Cervantes, Sasha Khokha, and Bobbie Murray, "Hate Unleashed: Los Angeles in the Aftermath of Proposition 187," *Chicana/o Latina/o Law Review* 17, no. 1 (1995), https://escholarship.org/uc/item/1p41v152.

7. Daniel B. Wood, "California's Prop. 187 Puts Illegal Immigrants on Edge," *Christian Science Monitor*, November 22, 1994, https://www.csmonitor.com/1994/1122/22021.html.

8. "Prop. 187 Approved in California," *Migration News* 1, no. 11 (December 1994), https://migration.ucdavis.edu/mn/more.php?id=492.

better understand what it is like to be undocumented. These families welcomed me into their lives and bravely shared their struggles. They took me to the fields where they picked fruit in the blistering heat. I tried to pick the fruit too; within minutes, my fingers bled from the thorns and my eyes stung from sweat and the pesticides in the air. This was their life, day in and day out. I met with their children. Over tamales and burritos, they shared their challenges with me. I listened to girls so smart and kind, any institution would be lucky to have them, yet they didn't qualify for financial aid. Their futures are a wild unknown, all because their parents chose to escape what were often critical conditions in their hometowns in the hopes of providing their children with more opportunities in life.

I also spent time discussing Lupe's story with the policy experts and leading immigration attorneys at the Criminal Justice Reform Program at Advancing Justice – Asian Law Caucus in San Francisco. They shared with me the reality that undocumented immigrants face today, which, as painful and hard as Prop 187 was, is even tougher now. Since President Trump took office, immigration arrests have gone up by 40 percent, at a rate of almost four hundred people a day.[9] All across the nation, families are being ripped apart. President Trump recently announced he was rescinding the Deferred Action for Childhood Arrivals (DACA) program, leaving the estimated 700,000 undocumented

9. Laurie Goodstein, "Immigrant Shielded From Deportation by Philadelphia Church Walks Free," *New York Times*, October 11, 2017, https://www.nytimes.com /2017/10/11/us/sanctuary-church-immigration-philadelphia.html?referer=https://t .co/T1OYHWcyJg?amp=1.

immigrant children in limbo, and possibly in danger of deportation.[10]

And while Lupe's dad, José, got a temporary stay, the immigration laws changed in 1996 such that it is significantly harder, almost impossible, for an undocumented person to gain legal status other than through marriage. Today, if Lupe's dad went before an immigration judge with the same set of circumstances, most likely he would be denied.

There are the notable cases where due to grassroots and community organization, deportations get postponed or canceled, such as the case of Javier Flores Garcia.[11] But they are the exception, not the norm. By not giving hardworking immigrants with no criminal convictions a realistic path to citizenship, undocumented immigrants are left fending for themselves in the dark, vulnerable to exploitation, abuse, misinformation, and hopelessness. My biggest hope in writing this book is that it will give people a better understanding of the circumstances facing undocumented immigrants so that we can enact better policy. Not just hot-button propositions to win elections, but laws that embody the vision and core values of our country.

10. Catherine E. Shoichet, Susannah Cullinane, and Tal Kopan, "US Immigration: DACA and Dreamers Explained," CNN.com, updated October 26, 2017, http://edition.cnn.com/2017/09/04/politics/daca-dreamers-immigration-program/index.html.
11. Goodstein, "Immigrant Shielded from Deportation."

ACKNOWLEDGMENTS

Three Keys was a book that took me many drafts to write, even though I've been living and breathing it for many years. I wanted to get the emotions of Mia and Lupe just right, because those feelings — worrying about one's immigration status, being pre-occupied by doubts and fears I couldn't say out loud to my class-mates but sat very much in the pit of my stomach, wondering whether I was "American enough," whether I was "too American," "not Chinese enough," "too Chinese" — were fears I had growing up, yet I never saw represented in any of the books I read.

In finding the courage to write about these experiences and finally giving voice to these emotions, I want to thank the following people, without whom this book would not exist:

First and foremost, my literary agent, Tina Dubois, who read and encouraged me with each draft. Every day, when I sit at my computer, pouring my most vulnerable self into my words, I picture you on the other end reading them, and it fills me with such comfort and joy. I'm so grateful to have you as my agent.

To my editor, Amanda Maciel, thank you for guiding me with each draft. Thank you for getting this story, getting the characters, and getting *me*. It is pure joy working with you. Your thoroughness and thoughtfulness, love of character, and ability to unlock what still needs to be done on a story with a single question blows me away. I am so lucky to have you as my editor — thank you for embracing this book with your whole heart.

To my greater Scholastic family: Talia Seidenfeld, my publisher David Levithan, my amazing publicist Lauren Donovan (LOVE YOU!), Ellie Berger, Erin Berger, Rachel Feld, Julia Eisler, Lizette Serrano, Emily Heddleson, and Danielle Yadao: Thank you so much for championing me and my books!

To Maike Plenzke and Maeve Norton, who once again did an *amazing* job with the cover!!! Maike, your cover art made Mia, Lupe, and Jason come to life in a way that took my breath away! I'm so so beyond grateful to get to work with you!!!

To John Schumacher, thank you for giving *Front Desk* such an enthusiastic, warm hug and booktalking it to librarians and kids all over the country!!! Your support means everything to me!!! Thank you for sharing your love of books with the world and championing reading and librarians!!!

To all the *Front Desk* fans, I am so humbled by the response to *Front Desk*, and I take the responsibility to carry on Mia's story very seriously. *Front Desk* was a book that got rejected by every publisher but Scholastic. The reason that *Three Keys* exists is because of YOU. Thank you to all the librarians and teachers who read, recommended, taught, and talked about *Front Desk* — you made this happen. Thank you for sending such a strong message that you want books about immigrants, that you CARE about diversity, and that kids from all walks of life deserve to see themselves represented in books.

As a teacher, some of the classroom scenes were heartbreaking to write, but they reflect the sentiment and mind-set of California at that time. I am grateful to my own elementary school teachers, who thankfully never treated me the way Mrs. Welch did. I am also grateful for my thirteen years in the classroom as a writing teacher and my dear friends and colleagues at the Kelly Yang Project, John Chew and Paul Smith, for their continued support and encouragement.

To my greater ICM team, John Burnham, Ava Greenfield, Roxane Edouard, Ron Bernstein, Bryan Diperstein, Alicia Gordon, Tamara Kawar, Morgan Woods, and Alyssa Weinberger, thank you for bringing me and my stories to the world. John, thank you for working tirelessly on my deals every day. I am honored to be one of your clients.

Thank you to my publishers around the globe — Walker Books, Kim Dong, Dipper, Omnibook, Editorial Lectura Colaborativa, and Porteghaal Publishing. To my lawyer, Richard Thompson, thank you for your wisdom and your guidance. Thank you for going on this wild journey with me. It comforts me so that I have you in my corner.

Many thanks to my dear friends and early readers Wayne Wang, Alan Gasmer, Ian Bryce, Irene Yeung, Peter Jaysen, and Alex Slater. A million thanks to Arthur Levine and Nick Thomas for acquiring this book. Major thanks as well to Yanelli Guerrero and Daniela Guerrero, as well as to Dr. Stephany Cuevas for reading and reviewing an early draft of *Three Keys*.

I am forever grateful to my dear friends Angela Chan and Anoop Prasad of the Asian Law Caucus for their knowledge and insight into immigration law. The Asian Law Caucus runs free legal clinics at their center in San Francisco every week in the areas of immigration, particularly deportation, housing, workers' rights, criminal justice, national security, and civil rights. If you or a relative are experiencing legal issues surrounding immigration and need assistance, please contact (415) 896-1701 or go to: advancingjustice-alc.org.

To my family, particularly my mom and dad, who came to this country with $200 in their pockets and toiled day and night so I might have a better future. Thank you for stepping bravely into the unknown with me and keeping me warm with love throughout all the ups and downs. To my kids, Eliot, Tilden, and Nina, thank you for cheering Mommy on. Eliot, thank you for reading *every* draft of *Three Keys* and telling me your thoughts on each one.

To my husband, Steve, thanks for listening to my stories and always making me feel like I'm the most entertaining girl in the room. ☺ To my dear friend and mentor, Paul Cummins, thank you for inspiring us all. I cherish our friendship deeply.

Finally, I would like to thank my school librarians. I am living, walking proof in the power of librarians to change lives. In *Three Keys*, Mia's school lets go of their school librarian due to budget cuts, and Mia suffers immensely in the aftermath. I put that scene in because I am profoundly worried about budget cuts affecting librarians, because if it weren't for school librarians, I would not be here today.

I hope my books bring hope and comfort to children of all different backgrounds and walks of life, just as the librarians in my school brought me.